A Pigeon From Calais

– BETH ROWLANDS –

An environmentally friendly book printed and bound in England
by www.printondemand-worldwide.com

Mixed Sources
Product group from well-managed
forests, and other controlled sources
www.fsc.org Cert no. TT-COC-002641
© 1996 Forest Stewardship Council
FSC

PEFC Certified
This product is
from sustainably
managed forests
and controlled
sources
PEFC/16-33-415 www.pefc.org

This book is made entirely of chain-of-custody materials

www.fast-print.net/store.php

A PIGEON FROM CALAIS
Copyright © Beth Rowlands 2014

The people in this story are fictitious except for four historical figures: the
Countess of Warwick, her daughters and the Vicar of Northleach.
They may or may not have had the characteristics portrayed here.
There is a list of characters at the end.

Cover: Colour, Cotswold Stone by eve dunlop Photography.
Drawings by the author.

ISBN 978-178456-018-8

First published 2014 by
FASTPRINT PUBLISHING
Peterborough, England.

To the memory of my teachers:
Richard Brayshaw and
Ivan Gray
who loved a story,

Barry Davies
who loved Northleach Church

Illustration by Nell Burditt

1469

Chapter 1
MIDDLEHAM CASTLE, YORKSHIRE

Anne is sitting at the table, drawing. Her sister, Isabel, throws more wood on the fire, puts a taper to the flame and lights the candles. Lydia is kneeling by an open chest looking at small possessions, choosing which to give to her friends and packing the rest into a basket. All three are holding fast to each moment of to-day, reluctant to face the parting to-morrow.

"Dost thou have to go to-morrow, Lyddie?" Anne says. "If thou stay'st one more week thou canst see my new pony."

"Thou know'st I have to go," Lydia replies. "Thy father has made all the arrangements and my father is expecting me."

"Well, why shouldn't I go with thee?" Anne has run out of all reasonable ideas for detaining her friend.

Lydia laughs. "And miss seeing thy new pony?" She puts her arm round Anne's shoulders. "What's this thou'rt drawing?"

"It's a picture of Middleham Castle for thy father. It's almost finished. Will he like it?"

"Oh, he will. And I think it will help me explain to him what it's like living here."

Isabel kneels on the floor, busy with a box of Lydia's.

"I've painted thy name on the box," she says to Lydia. "Is there anything else to go in it?"

"Let's see if Anne's drawing will fit." Lydia passes the picture to Isabel to try for size. It will go in comfortably. Anne busies herself with the finishing touches.

For the last five years Lydia Woolman has lived as

one of the family of the Earl and Countess of Warwick. She is close in age to Isabel and has shared her lessons, while Anne is only thirteen.

They have spent much of their time here, when not out walking or riding, in the old schoolroom high up by the battlements of Middleham Castle. The room is shabby and the furniture old; all their books are here and materials for painting and needlework and their musical instruments. But now everything will change. The family has to go to London and Lydia, now so nearly grown up, needs to return to her father in Northleach in Gloucestershire. Lydia says, "I'll write to thee Anne, and next time you come to Warwick Castle we can all have a day together." She puts various small objects into a bag and hands it to Isabel. "If this'll go in the box, then I think we've finished."

The family's living quarters are on the west side of the buildings ranged round the old keep of the castle. They were improved by the present earl's grandfather, Ralph Neville, Earl of Westmorland, in the fourteen-twenties. The rooms are reached from the courtyard by a staircase in the Garderobe Tower. Water and firewood are daily brought up these stairs by numerous servants. The family apartment is connected to the upper part of the keep by a bridge. This leads first to the Great Chamber, and next, to the Great Hall. Here breakfast and dinner are served to all the castle-dwellers. As well as the family, there are numerous stewards and officials and also the young men in training for service to the earl, including the king's young brother, Richard of Gloucester. With the company assembled for the meal the senior steward calls for silence, the earl says Grace and then the hubbub breaks out.

The young men joke, their voices rising; kitchen maids bustle up from below with steaming dishes, the lids clatter on the tables. More servants gather up empty plates and pots to carry down a different staircase to avoid collisions.

At other times refreshments are brought to the family's apartment. The countess particularly values these quieter times when she can relax and enjoy the chatter of her girls and listen to her husband's plans for the next day.

The girls hear footsteps on the stairs. The door opens and the countess comes in with a young maid, Connie. "Lydia, my dear, is the packing finished? I've come to say farewell. I hope to see thee off in the morning but there'll be such a bustle with so many people leaving all at once." She embraces Lydia.

"Goodbye dear Mam, I can never thank you enough for all your kindness."

"Thou know'st what a good friend thy dear mother was to me, Lyddie. I know she would be proud of thee. I have a little present for thee, here."

The maid hands the countess a box she is carrying and helps her remove the lid. The countess takes out two small pictures and gives them to Lydia.

"Oh Madam! The paintings of the girls that were done last year! Can you really spare them?"

"They're for thee, my dear. I have the originals to look at."

"Oh, thank you. I shall treasure them."

Lydia looks tenderly at the two pictures. Neither girl is a beauty but the artist has conveyed much of their sweetness and vitality. Isabel's colouring is muted, with light brown hair and grey eyes; Anne's more striking, her blue eyes setting off her dark hair.

Isabel is standing by Lydia and takes the pictures from her for packing. Anne is working hard on appearing not to be there.

Her mother is well aware of this. "Now Annie, say goodnight and be off to bed."

"Mama! It's Lydia's last evening. Please let me stay up."

"If thou goest not now, thou'll oversleep in the morning and miss waving goodbye."

Anne gives Lydia the finished drawing and hugs her tight. "Oh Lyddie, goodnight. Thou'lt not forget us wilt thou?"

"How could I? I shall look at your portraits every day and write often."

"Every week? I promise I shall write every week." They hug again and Lydia hugs Connie too. The two set off down the stairs and Anne's goodbyes gradually fade.

Isabel smiles at her mother. "Thank thee Mama, I haven't had a moment with Lydia all day."

"Have an hour together now. But don't talk too late; Lydia will need her rest." She embraces both girls before leaving them alone.

Isabel pours milk from a pitcher into two cups and they sit down at the table.

"How kind of thy mother," Lydia says. "The pictures are lovely."

"I'm glad thou like'st them. All I have of thee is the little one I painted last winter."

"It's a good painting but it makes me look very serious."

"Lyddie, we need to be serious for a minute. I'm worried about Father."

"Is it his quarrel with the king?"

"Yes, I've discovered why the king's marriage made Father so angry. We all knew he was disappointed that King Edward had found a Lancastrian widow none of us knew, for his bride. I now know that Father was abroad negotiating for the hand of a French princess at the time and the king kept his secret for three months before Father found out."

"So that's what happened."

"Yes. I was talking to one of Mother's women yesterday. She told me. She was surprised I hadn't realised. I was only about twelve at the time and not interested in such things."

"It must have offended my lord deeply."

"He finds it hard to forgive. And now he is trying to persuade George of Clarence to marry me in defiance of the king."

"George is quite keen isn't he? And how about thee?"

"We're good friends. I think it will have to be, Lyddie. But I'd much rather wait a year or so. It makes me uneasy that Father is no longer friends with George's brother the king."

There is nothing more Lydia can say. George of Clarence is heir to the throne, for the king has three daughters but no son. Lydia knows George to be good company with a kindly and cheerful disposition. At the same time she suspects he is rather too full of his own importance and too lazy to have benefited much from his education. He is tall and handsome like his brother, a skilled horseman and keen huntsman. But in Lydia's eyes he is not worthy of a wife such as Isabel.

Isabel rises and goes to a chest to take out a book. "I've been trying to tell thee all day. I've finished the copy of the message book for you and started one for Anne. We each have exactly the same and we must all stick to our promise to keep our secret safe."

Laughing, Lydia says, "Thou think'st we'll still need our private code?"

But Isabel is not laughing. "I just have a feeling we may need to tell each other private things. It makes me feel safer. I'll speak seriously to Anne about it when she's a bit older."

"I promise I'll keep it safe." Lydia puts the book into her box.

They chatter on, speculating what Isabel's life will be like in London and Lydia's in Northleach and promise that they will always be friends in spite of the big difference in their positions in life.

"Thou'll write, won't thou?" Lydia says. "Thou

know'st my father has messengers all the time going between Northleach and London on wool business so it'll be much easier than getting letters from Middleham."

"Thou must let me know the address of thy father's agent in London," Isabel says, and yawning, "I shall have to start my own packing tomorrow."

"We'd better get to bed."

"I'll be up early to see thee go."

They each take up a candle and go down the winding stair to their rooms, wishing each other sound sleep.

Lydia makes ready for bed but then, pulling her shawl round her shoulders, stands at the open window looking out from the castle across the moors, the humped shapes just visible in the starlight. She tries to feel brave about the huge change that will come to her now. She feels like clinging to the familiar people and customs of castle life but there is no part for her here as she reaches adulthood.

What lies ahead for Isabel? Lydia knows that her friend will have a harder role than hers; she shrinks from the thought of marriage to a royal prince. But Isabel is devoted to her father and willing to accept his guidance. At least Isabel knows George of Clarence and enjoys his company. He seems to have no serious shortcomings. But Lydia doesn't think Isabel's heart is stirred by George. The girls have read many romantic tales of ardent lovers arriving too late and Lydia dreads this for Isabel. She herself is heart-whole.

She has looked around the Great Hall at Middleham many times when there are guests gathered for a feast and decided that when she chooses a husband he will be tall and dark with smiling eyes. The few who qualify are always gone on the morrow. Perhaps...

She shivers, turns to the bed, blows out the candle and settles into a deep sleep.

Chapter 2
LYDIA'S JOURNEY

At last they reached Warwick Castle and, although tantalisingly near home, Lydia was glad of a good rest. She had to stay there several days because the party of men from Middleham was going no farther and a man to accompany her the remaining miles could not be spared at once.

She could remember visiting the castle briefly with the family some years before. On the more recent travels of the earl and countess they had taken only Isabel; Anne preferred to stay at Middleham and Lydia had stayed too, to keep her company.

Middleham now seemed far away and she felt a slight insecurity, a kind of limbo, as she found she belonged nowhere. Northleach was distant too. She had only a hazy memory of her father's appearance and a few images of the town with her home in the Market Place.

Everything at Warwick was strange and temporary. She missed Isabel and Anne; so many comments and jokes for them had come to her as she travelled and she could not share them. But her mind had been mainly occupied by the constant interest in the scenes she had passed through. The strangeness of the beds in the inns along the way hadn't bothered her, falling as she did each night into an exhausted sleep. The weather had continued mainly fine and on the one wet day they had, a halt was called early so that all the travellers could dry their clothes and the horses could be rubbed down and rested.

Spring had unfolded rapidly as they travelled south, the hedges baring as they climbed on to higher ground and greening again in the valleys. Here in Warwickshire the green, rolling, tree-studded pastureland delighted Lydia in its contrast with Middleham's high moors.

All the servants at the castle were devoted to the countess and her daughters so made a great fuss of Lydia, asking her for news of the Neville girls and curious about the different life she would live from now on. Of that she could tell them little but she enjoyed their fussing. A hot bath relieved her aches and some gentle walking eased her saddle-soreness. The servants showed her every fascinating nook and cranny of the castle except for the earl's most private rooms. There were no prisoners in the dungeon but all the possibilities of different degrees of punishment were displayed for her.

Those of the younger people who were literate devised games and competitions to amuse her, explaining the many ideas Isabel had taught them which brought her friend vividly to her mind. Her clothes were washed and mended and new ones found for her according to Isabel's instructions.

On the fifth day she was told to prepare herself for the morrow when Christopher, a tall, quiet man, together with a boy, Nat, were charged with seeing her home; they were to continue with messages for Bristol. Lydia was seen off as if of noble family and settled herself on the fresh horse with a comfortable feeling of being an experienced traveller ready for anything. They had forty miles to cover, a longer day's ride than most they had accomplished so far. The packhorse, now even more heavily loaded, could not make a fast pace. On arrival in Northleach, he would rest at an inn and later take a place in the wool train. Lydia's new mount, selected by the castle's head groom as a gift from the earl for her father, was a little impatient, but as they grew accustomed to each other, became obedient.

After crossing the River Windrush the old road climbed steadily up but dipped again into three more valleys. The horses were tiring, so on the last ascent the riders walked. Christopher and Nat transferred a pannier to each mount to give the packhorse some relief.

"Your home is in the next valley, Miss Lydia," Christopher said. "Do you remember anything of the road?"

She told him it was five years since she had left home and she could remember nothing. There were sheep and lambs to be seen on the pastures. The birds were still singing as lustily as they had sung all day. For several miles they had travelled with the sun in their eyes; it was a relief now that it was nearing the west. The journey assumed a dreamlike quality. She could not quite imagine what it would be like to see her father in their home so soon now; it was hard to believe that the journeying would not go on for ever.

When at last they turned off the main road into the town, the scenes before her stirred memories. Lydia became animated, pointing out to the men a familiar house and a place by the brook where she had played as a young child.

Chapter 3
"IF PLENTEY CAN GIVE..."

"If Plentey can give another ten pounds to the church, then so can I," Richard Woolman said to his oldest friend, Simon Trencher.

It was a fresh morning after a night's rain. Richard had tired of his counting house and had brought out two fells to spread on the old bench under the apple tree. The two men sat over a cup of ale and talked over local matters. Both had been widowed years before and were of kindly support to one another. Richard had learned from Simon the present state of the church rebuilding fund.

"It's good of thee, Richard, thank thee," Simon replied.

"Maybe it's not such a generous impulse after all. A church should be built for love of God, not to satisfy a man's pride."

"The church will be there long after we are gone," said Simon. "Only God will know which man gave from a truly generous heart."

"Or in thankfulness for the enjoyment of earthly pleasure, or in hope of escaping purgatory, or in guilt at failing to help the poor and needy. Do we have a single pure motive for what we do?" His tone was gently mocking and his friend smiled.

"I know thou lov'st our church, Richard. I will tell the other churchwardens of thy gift."

Richard Woolman was one of Northleach's wool merchants, his father and grandfather having built up the business before him. He ran a large flock of sheep and employed four shepherds to tend them, helped by five boys. He owned a big wool store, four horses, a cote full of pigeons, six laying hens and the old dog lying at his feet. There were two servants in the house, Margery, his housekeeper who had worked faithfully for many years, and Tim, a young lad he was training to assist him in the household and the business. He also had the help of a stable-hand and a man who planted vegetables for him in the spring.

Richard was a medium-sized man of stocky build, quiet, good-humoured and unassuming. In matters other than business he was sometimes a little unsure of himself.

Simon was taller than Richard, with fair hair thinning on top. He was the town baker and managed his business with one apprentice to help him. "I must be off soon," he said, "but I came hoping to have a glimpse of Lydia. How did she find the journey from Middleham?"

"She rested yesterday but she was up early this morning, asking questions. Joshua has taken her out to see the sheep."

"The life here must seem strange to her after what she's been used to."

"She seemed like a stranger to me - for about an hour! But because *she* remembered *me* we soon became like old friends."

Richard didn't yet feel ready to tell his companion how startled he had been when he went to his door and saw a young woman dismount. He had been looking out for Lydia all day but for a moment it was as if his dead wife had travelled back to him. The woman had turned towards him with a familiar gesture and smiled a well-remembered smile. She had then introduced the man and the boy accompanying her and, suddenly shy, had come to him for his embrace. He had folded her to him while he gathered his wits and then held her at arm's length to get to see the dear face of the one who was, after all, his daughter and had his own brown eyes and not her mother's blue ones.

The men heard footsteps and Richard Woolman went to the yard gate to find John Plentey trying to open it. "John, come in! What can I do for you?"

John Plentey was another of the merchants of the town. They enjoyed a friendly rivalry. "Good day Richard, Simon," he said. "I'm out on my rounds and before going home I hoped to see your lass."

"Lydia's out looking at the sheep. She'll be back shortly. Come and join us."

Plentey sat down by Trencher while Woolman perched on the end of a low wall. "And what could she tell you about your namesake, Richard, Earl of Warwick?" John Plentey asked.

"All I've heard is that the king has given Warwick command of the fleet and that he has to be a great deal in the Channel ports and in Calais," Richard replied.

"The king has no option. Warwick owns the greater number of ships," remarked Simon.

"Well, for all Warwick's power and ambition, he's a generous man. I shall always be grateful for all he's done for Lydia. I would do anything for my Lord of Warwick and his family," Richard replied.

Lydia had now returned home and, hearing voices at the back, came out to the garden. She approached the men a little shyly, surprised to find her father had company. She greeted them politely as her father introduced them. "Hast thou counted the lambs?" her father asked.

"I think Joshua did. I've been to see the horses too." Lydia had a distant memory of a much younger Joshua, living in the house. He had carried out the duties which now were Tim's.

"And the pigeons, Father. I didn't realise thou hadst so many."

"Yes, they've multiplied over the last two years. My friends wonder that I spend so much time and trouble over them."

"Where didst thou get the idea, Father?"

"A merchant in Antwerp who has long been buying my wool, sent me a pigeon in a basket, by Calais and London. He asked me to send my answer to his letter, fixed to the bird's leg and to release it on a calm day an hour before noon. The pigeon reached Antwerp before nightfall and my friend had his answer."

"How amazing it knew where to go," Lydia said.

"They have a rare intelligence. A few weeks later a present of two young birds arrived, with instructions for their care. I could fatten them for the pot or breed more birds for pies and pots. But if I could spare the time and trouble, chicks could be trained as homing pigeons like his."

"Thou couldn'st put such special birds in the pot, Father!"

"That's what Joshua said. He was here when they arrived and begged me to allow him to care for them and study how to train them. Joshua has bred many chicks from the first pair and this year we have fifteen trained for a long-distance flight."

"Your father has been generous and sent pigeons with my messages too," John said. "Now Richard, I must be going," and he wished them good day.

As he opened the gate he nearly bumped into a girl approaching Woolman's house. It was Trencher's daughter, Ellen. She was an attractive lass with fair hair, more slightly built than Lydia but almost as tall.

Woolman had now reached the gate.

"Mr Woolman, is my father here? Oh, Father, there's a man from the mill come to see thee and I thought thou mightst be here."

Woolman said, "Come in Ellen. You must meet Lydia. I believe you remember her?"

"Yes, I do. Hullo, Lydia! I heard you were coming. I hope you'll be happy in Northleach."

Lydia greeted Ellen and invited her to sit with her on the bench. Simon excused himself, but encouraged Ellen to stay a little.

"I'll walk with thee, Simon," said Richard.

The two girls sat down and Lydia told Ellen she remembered her as quite a little girl and Ellen told Lydia that she had seemed quite a big girl and they discovered there were two years between them in age.

"Father told me that you've been a companion to my Lord of Warwick's daughter," said Ellen.

"Yes, the family needs to be in London and Calais now. My lord plans to find a husband for Isabel."

"She's almost eighteen like you, isn't she? Does she want to be married so young?"

"She's known for some time that it's expected of her."

"And the younger girl?"

"Anne is five years younger than Isabel. Would you like to see some of the keepsakes they gave me?" Lydia led the way indoors. The gifts were still on the table where she had been showing them to her father.

"This is one of Anne's drawings. Oh, and this lovely manuscript was a treasure of Isabel's and she gave it me. Look at the beautiful writing!"

"But Lydia, I can't read!"

"Oh, I'm so sorry - there, I've been insensitive already."

"No matter. But you have had a very unusual life, sharing Isabel's education, haven't you? I can write my name and figures for adding up, of course, and I can recognise just a few words if they're written clearly."

Lydia said, "Would you let me teach you? Is reading something you would like to do?"

"Oh yes! I have tried sometimes. We have a primer at home. It's in Latin but one of my uncles has written verses in English in the blank spaces. I've tried to puzzle them out, but the writing is very small and I'm so often called away to do something more useful."

"I'm sure I could help you. You could bring the primer and I'll copy out a verse or two in larger writing. When can you come round?"

"The early morning is best. Father is up at four o'clock and doesn't need me for the baking, but later on I have to be in the shop."

"I'll ask my father if I can start in the counting house at eight and you could come at seven."

They parted, agreeing to meet again next morning. Lydia gathered up her treasures and took them up to the little room she remembered more than any other in the house, where she had slept as a young child. She loved to look from her window above the eaves and see the townsfolk going about the market place. She began to write a letter to Isabel and Anne while the time at Warwick was still fresh in her mind. She had already hung their portraits above her table.

Tomorrow she was to start helping her father with his account books and records. He had suggested that she have the afternoons to herself while she got used to Northleach and she realised she would be quite free to come and go. How Isabel would love that... and yet... Isabel had grown up knowing her place was in a noble family where always someone would be watching.

She recalled the days last summer when, with the earl away, the countess had decided to allow the three girls to run free. Always before, a man from the castle had been ordered to accompany them on their outings with the ponies and dogs, keeping a discreet distance but responsible for their safety. Later, Lydia and Isabel realised that the countess had memories of her own tomboy childhood and knew that they could be trusted as she had been. Anne, Countess of Warwick, knew how precious freedom was and that her daughters might never taste it again. She was loved by all the country folk and always felt safe among them.

On that first day out alone, Isabel, Lydia and Anne had been astonished by the decision and determined to keep the bounds set them and not be late back. They knew the surroundings of the castle well and that it would be foolish to go far beyond the familiar territory.

They found a dip in the moor, just off the usual track, with a small, fast-flowing brook. Three rowan trees gave a patch of shade making it a good place to rest the ponies. Isabel suggested they make a pool so as to drink more easily and they set about building a miniature dam with stones and moss and heather. Anne stood in the pool scooping up water in her cupped hands; the bigger girls teased her for cooling her feet in the water she drank from, like a bird. They were splashed with water in return and, laughing and exhausted, all three lay on the bank, their clothes drying in the sun while they ate the bread and cheese they had brought with them. Then they allowed the dogs to lap at the pool. They moved into the shade and lay in the bracken taking turns to tell fanciful stories until Isabel announced it was time to start for home. When the girls had had a last drink they brought the ponies down to take their turn.

Lydia decided that this afternoon, she would try to make a friend of the stableman.

Chapter 4
THE VICAR OF NORTHLEACH

Early on a spring morning, the sun streaming in despite the dust on the east window of the chancel, the Vicar knelt in prayer. His name was Geoffrey Langbroke. He had knelt here every morning of the past eleven years and he knew and loved all the people of Northleach.

He was forty years old, a tall man of lean build with a kindly disposition. He kept most of his opinions to himself while he listened to the stories of woe or joy the people brought him. He preached with conviction and his hearers knew he tried to practise the message himself.

He had taken the vows of a monk as a young man in St Peter's Abbey in Gloucester and for several years was certain that he was called to the monastic life. In reading widely and acquainting himself with the affairs of the world he began to see that he was becoming lazy and valuing the life of the abbey as a safe refuge rather than as a challenge to his talents. Gradually the certainty grew that he should offer himself as vicar to a parish.

When the Abbot sent for Geoffrey and told him that a pastor was needed at Northleach, a small town in the hills, he had to work hard to hide his disappointment. He had seen himself perhaps still in Gloucester or in one of the outlying parishes, or in another great city. He knew nothing of small town life, of hill farmers and rural tradespeople. He had grown up in Gloucester in a street teeming with people near the wharves where he had spent his free

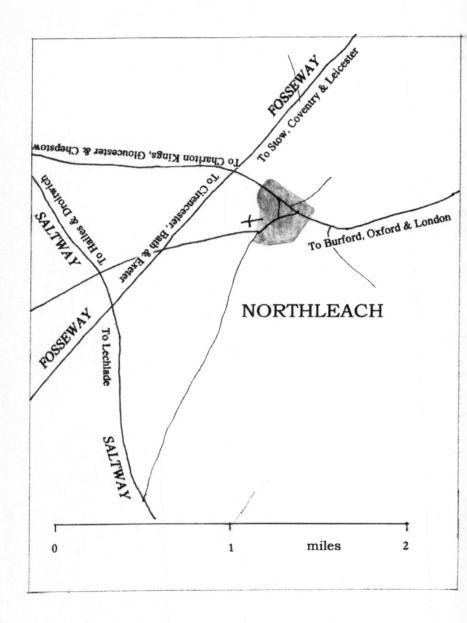

FOSSEWAY

To Stow, Coventry & Leicester

To Charlton Kings, Gloucester & Chepstow

To Cirencester, Bath & Exeter

To Halles & Droitwich

SALTWAY

FOSSEWAY

To Lechlade

To Burford, Oxford & London

NORTHLEACH

SALTWAY

0   1   miles   2

time watching the ships and sailors and dockers.

Arrived in Northleach, he quickly became absorbed in his new life, fascinated that there could be a complete civilisation other than that of a city. He was at first surprised to find that the little town, far from being a backwater, a quiet settlement in the middle of nowhere, was the hub, first of a trading community and then of the whole transport system of England. Gradually Gloucester faded in memory to a place on the edge of the world, almost in barbarous Wales.

Northleach town had been granted its charter in 1227. Earlier it had been a place of a few cottages round a mill. Now the church was extended and domestic plots - burgages - were laid out round a market place. Villagers from five miles round and more brought their produce and animals here for sale. Most of the villages had their own baker, carpenter, blacksmith and weaver. But on market day, which was Wednesday, the services of miller, butcher and brewer, farrier and harness maker, wheelwright, cobbler and chandler were sought. The villages, Farmington, Eastington, Coln Rogers, Yanworth, Haselton, Notgrove, Turkdean and Hampnett were set in the rolling hills of the headwaters of Windrush, Leach and Coln that fed the Thames.

The Vicar's substantially-built house stood on the bank of the River Leach, above the mill. Established wool merchants and craftsmen had each his own stone-built house and burgage plot. Most kept a pig and fowls or bees and ran a few sheep, as did many of the cottagers. Some paid a large part of their tithes in pork and eggs; at times the Vicar was overwhelmed with these provisions and would pay a boy - in pork, of course - to ride on his own horse to Gloucester to take the goods to the abbey for the poor and needy.

As a monk he had been accustomed to taking his

turn in kitchen, laundry and garden but now that his good people met his every need, his labour was to visit the poor and sick and this nourished his prayers. For recreation he visited or invited the vicars from the country parishes, as varied a set of men as you could find anywhere, one or two of them studious and well-read like himself, one almost illiterate, just able to write his name and to read the gospel and epistle in Latin on a Sunday because he knew the words by heart; all were united in their devotion to the Master and strengthened by their fellowship.

The church was of considerable size for a small town. Over a hundred years ago a great tower had been built and a beautiful porch with a room above it. This had made the nave seem old-fashioned, stunted even, so plans were made to rebuild that too, with high clerestorey windows to let in light. At first there was little money to be found. Gradually, some of the more prosperous citizens, seeing finer churches when their business took them to Chipping Campden and Cirencester, began to plan how Northleach church could outshine them all. By 1445 they were ready to pay for the old columns to be demolished so that rebuilding might begin. When Geoffrey arrived in the town the new columns and clerestorey windows were nearly complete but still more money was needed for the roof.

The roof was finished now; no more damage could be caused by rain. Yet, still more work was needed.

Geoffrey was at first amazed by the crowds of travellers in the town. The four inns competed to give the best service and resting place for both man and horse. All had ample room for horses and were able to provide fresh ones for folk in a hurry. Where could they all be going? And why was their journey so urgent and necessary?

He soon realised that local people often needed to

visit Burford, Cirencester or Stow, perhaps to seek a lawyer, silversmith or glover, and that a day's ride could take one not only to Gloucester but to Oxford, Bath, Worcester or Coventry, while it was but ninety miles to London. The greatest press of traffic occurred at the times of the horse fairs in Stow and Charlton Kings.

In spring and summer a constant stream of pilgrims passed by on the Fosseway, heading south-west for Bristol where they could take ship for St Iago de Compostela. Others took the opposite direction making for Hailes Abbey which housed the relic of the blood of Jesus.

An ancient saltway passed nearby, the loaded horses and mules carrying salt to Lechlade to be taken by boat to London. They came from Droitwich, near Worcester, and climbed out of the vale either at Hailes or Broadway, skirting the heads of the valleys. The road kept its straight line until interrupted by a loop of the River Coln which had to be negotiated before the travellers could reach the River Thames at Lechlade, near the place where it was joined by the River Leach.

The Vicar rose from his prayers and turned to find Simon Trencher standing quietly waiting to speak to him.

"What a lovely morning, Sir Geoffrey."

"Simon! Good morning to you. I was hoping to see you today."

"I have come to bring Tom the latest figures."

Tom was the Foreman of the building work. He could just be heard at the other end of the church giving orders to Joshua, his right-hand man, and two of the labourers. He began to walk towards the chancel, calling over his shoulder as he came, "Now get on with it lads, I want all that finished by midday. And Joshua, tell me if you find anything up there." Joshua could be seen making for the stairway that led to the roof.

The three men exchanged greetings and the Vicar told Simon and Tom that he was expecting Brother Walter to ride over from the abbey at Gloucester today to find out how the work on the church was going.

"Come into the nave, sir," Tom said. "We've just completed the glazing of the new windows. We'll be taking the scaffolding down next week."

The Vicar peered up through the scaffolding. "The windows look good, Tom. So I can tell him that we can safely have lighted candles in the nave at last... and what else shall I say?"

"The churchwardens agreed, didn't they, Mr Trencher? The work on the south aisle and porch should be left to be finished later. All of old Mr Plentey's money has been spent on the nave."

"We've had more legacies recently so we can definitely finish the north aisle next, Tom."

"Yes, sir. The men have just started work on it. And we'll be starting the floor paving for the whole church during the autumn."

"Will we be ready for a service in the nave by next spring?" the Vicar asked Tom.

"Can't promise, sir, it depends what men I can get and how many ideas the churchwardens have about the floor, eh Mr Trencher?"

"Quite so, Tom."

"How many men have we working at the moment?" the Vicar asked.

"Two masons carving figures. Four labourers and three carpenters. The team of woodcarvers is still at work on the rood screen of course. It was stacked in sections in Mr Swift's barn a good many years ago. I have Joshua always in and out who can turn his hand to anything. He's up on the nave roof now trying to find a leak."

Joshua reappeared at this point. He was a big, strong man, quietly spoken and diligent. Both his parents had died when he was very young. Richard Woolman had taken him in, employed him as a servant and then apprenticed him to a mason. He was a reliable laying-mason but with no particular gift for carving stone. His passion was animals and he would help out with the sheep or horses whenever needed. He had also been quick to understand the workings of the great crane which had been necessary to lift the heavy blocks of stone. When at last its work was done, it was Joshua's ingenuity and patience that had found a way to get it out of the church. It stood, still, at the back of the churchyard, leaning against one of the great trees and securely roped to it. Tom could remember Joshua's father, Amos, whom Joshua had barely known. It had been said of him, 'There's nothing that man can't do, with a horse and a length of chain'.

Joshua had established a routine now where he would assist Tom daily after calling round first to help Woolman.

"Good morning, Vicar, morning Mr Trencher," said Joshua. "I've found where the water was getting in, Tom."

"See if you can patch it up, lad. I'll get the plumbers to check it when they come back to do the leadwork on the north aisle."

When Joshua was out of earshot Tom said, "I don't know what I'd do without that lad. I'm not going up steps and ladders much meself since that bit of trouble with me foot, but I can trust Joshua to explain to me exactly what he finds. He's a good mason too and always here, in Northleach."

"Mr Woolman is surely needing him at this time of the year?" the Vicar said.

"Not until shearing begins. Then I'll not see much of him for a while, though I expect he'll look in for a moment most days."

"I must be getting back to the bakery," Trencher said. "Here are the figures for you to check Tom," and to the Vicar, "I'll see you this afternoon, sir."

"God go with you, Simon."

Tom looked at the papers Simon Trencher had given him. When materials were delivered for the building work, he kept the delivery notes carefully for the churchwardens who later paid the bills and received the receipts. The churchwardens liked Tom to see the records they made when they were completed and check that nothing was left out. Tom was only thankful that he did not have to do the writing himself. He knew these details were necessary but he had enough on his hands trying to find sources for some of the materials he required and checking the men's worksheets and paying the wages.

He had lived all his life in a small house near the church. Everyone knew him as Tom and any other name he may have had was unknown to his neighbours. His father had been foreman before him and had had the boy apprenticed to a mason when very young, subsequently requiring him to spend some time with every other tradesman on the site. He was cherished by everyone in Northleach, a fact which brought him some comfort in his loneliness. His wife and sons had died some years before; he had reached the age of fifty and suffered considerable pain in one leg following a heavy fall, so that he walked with a slight limp. It was his relaxed disposition combined with a strong determination to hire only the best workers and to aim for the completion of the finest church building in the county that endeared him to the people of Northleach. He was tolerant of all opinions and had a detached scepticism regarding the power of prayer. This he kept to himself as he had a genuine respect for the Vicar.

He was thankful the winter was over and encouraged by the recent progress in the building work. He had a good complement of craftsmen who

had worked together over a month now.
Each morning he came eagerly to work.

Chapter 5
DINNER AT THE WOOLMANS

John Plentey was perplexed. Last night a traveller stopping at the King's Head on his way to Chepstow had told him the news from London. It was being said that Richard Neville, the great Earl of Warwick, was again defying King Edward the Fourth.

The season of shipping wool to Calais had just begun. Calais was an important port and English possession. The earl was Captain of the Calais garrison. Might the king appoint someone else instead? Could there even be a blockade of Calais? Plentey shuddered at the thought. Surely that was unlikely. Both men understood the port's significance. He recalled his father's anxiety some twenty years ago when the king had been short of funds to pay the men of the garrison. The soldiers had impounded large quantities of wool. The merchants had gone unpaid and had to wait for months for business to resume.

When John Plentey called at Richard Woolman's house he found that Richard's cousin, Adam Fry, had just arrived from London.

"Come back in an hour, John," Richard said. "Join us for dinner and you shall hear all the gossip from the City." He enquired whether Mrs Plentey would like to come too. John said she was a little unwell and needed a quiet day at home but that she would be pleased if Lydia would call on her in the next few days.

John Plentey's grandfather had sent much of his wool to Italy, shipping it from Southampton, but nowadays it all had to go to the Continent through Calais where the merchants of the Staple collected the tax for the king. All the wool merchants kept a store of wool through the winter ready to ship to the Whitsun markets in Bruges, Antwerp and Ghent, as soon as the spring storms at sea died down. The storehouses must be cleared before sheep shearing began in June.

Adam Fry was a merchant of the Staple and usually made the arrangements for Richard Woolman's wool to be shipped. He came every year at this time to see the wool and assess its quality, before sending his packers down to Northleach. Richard often arranged a dinner for his friends, to meet his cousin.

John Plentey walked home, still perturbed about the Earl of Warwick. If only he could have swallowed his pride and worked under the young man he had helped to the throne. He had guided and befriended King Edward in the days after the death in battle of his father and brother and later fought bravely for him.

But now that the king was older, and more sure of his importance, he was pursuing his own policies whether or not they met with the approval of the earl. John recalled the time, not many years ago, when Warwick was away in France negotiating for a bride for Edward, unaware that the king had secretly married a beautiful widow who had formerly been at the Lancastrian king's court. This had been the first setback to Warwick's influence.

When John Plentey returned he was welcomed in by Lydia. Simon Trencher was there already and Richard was pouring wine for them all, before sitting down to dinner. Lydia went to the kitchen where she was helping Margery prepare the meal.

"It's good to see your lass so much at home with you, Cousin," said Fry. "She must find living here very different from Middleham Castle!"

Richard smiled to himself. He was not going to tell his friends that at the end of Lydia's first week, he had realised that she spent more of her time in the stables than in the kitchen. When questioned she had told him that at the castle, when lessons were over, she and Isabel loved to visit the ponies and were forever grooming them, Anne tying ribbons in their manes. Children were not welcome in the kitchen which bustled with hierarchies of cooks, undercooks and scullions, many of them wielding sharp knives, butchering carcasses and disposing of entrails.

Lydia liked Margery and was only too willing to help. She quickly came to understand that she must be like a Northleach housewife, supervising all cooking and marketing and doing much of the work herself. Margery was glad of the company and began teaching her young mistress all she knew. How different it was for Isabel and Anne, thought Lydia. The countess would not expect her girls to do more than order meals when they had their own households. The countess herself had a particular skill in finding medicinal plants and treating the ailments of old and young who came to her; and she made it her business to visit the families around the castle to make sure that mothers-to-be had enough experienced women in the family to help them when their time came.

Woolman told his cousin, "Lydia's heard today that Isabel Neville will marry the king's brother, the Duke of Clarence."

"But I thought the Pope had refused a dispensation. They're cousins aren't they? And King Edward was against the match," said Plentey.

"The Pope has been persuaded. My Lord of Warwick's brother, the Archbishop of York, will perform the ceremony in Calais."

"So Warwick is defying the king!" Fry said.

"They've quarrelled before and made up. Only last month he was a guest of the king at Windsor," Plentey reminded him.

"I fear they will continue to quarrel, and I for one will support King Edward," said Fry, knowing that his cousin would always put the earl before the king.

Woolman said, "He is a strong and fair-minded king. Surely my lord has more sense than to quarrel with him again? He must put the peace of the realm first." But he sounded uneasy.

"There'll always be trouble while King Harry is a captive in the Tower," Fry observed.

Woolman wished his cousin had not brought that subject up; Simon Trencher was a supporter of the old Lancastrian king who, having lost his wits, was unfit to rule but was nevertheless king.

So Trencher put in his usual word, "I still support King Harry. He was anointed king as a child and I do not recognise that another king can be anointed and crowned by another archbishop while the first lives."

"But King Harry has been ill so long he cannot perform his duties," said Plentey.

Fry added, "Queen Marguerite is still hated for the misconduct and cruelty of her soldiers."

It was a never-ending argument round many tables in England. The Duke of York, King Edward's father, had made a claim to be King Henry's heir; it was bitterly disputed by Henry's French queen from the time her own son was born. The duke had been killed in a terrible battle in the north but eventually King Henry had been captured and Queen Marguerite had been driven back to France.

Adam Fry wouldn't drop the subject. "All the traders in London support King Edward," he said, "knowing he understands business."

Simon Trencher wouldn't drop it either. "I must put my loyalty to King Harry before trade and business," he said.

"That's easy for you to say, Trencher, your business is constant. A man may make his old woollen cloak last another winter but he will spend his last penny on bread!"

"Come now!" Plentey said. "We'll not quarrel in Richard's house. We can all agree we want what's best for England."

To Richard's relief, the Vicar arrived at this point and there was no more arguing for the evening. Lydia brought him into the room and offered him wine.

"Welcome, Sir Geoffrey," said Richard. "You know my cousin, Adam Fry, from London."

"Yes, yes, we met last year," said Geoffrey. "Good evening, Fry."

The others greeted the Vicar, who continued, "Are you in the Cotswolds long, Mr Fry?"

"It's a flying visit this time, sir. I came to examine my cousin's wool and tomorrow two of my men should arrive to start the packing. The wool train leaves next week. But I'll be back around the time of your St Peter and Paul Commemoration Service."

"I have only a few sheep but I hope you will offer me a price for my wool, sir," Geoffrey said.

"I should be glad to. The building work is going well at the church, I trust?"

"Yes, very well. I'd be pleased to show you round."

"We've been admiring the new clerestorey windows from the outside for years, but now at last we are allowed into the nave," Richard told him.

"It's good to see you so enthusiastic about it now, Richard. You were still full of doubts only last year," John said.

Richard smiled. "I wasn't the only one. But I was mainly worried about the snow that might collect on the nave roof; it's nearly flat." He turned to Adam, "In the Cotswolds it's traditional to make steep roofs of stone tiles for the snow to slide off."

"So how has the new roof stood up to the snow?"

"It's been up two winters now, and given no

trouble," Plentey replied. "The master carpenter told me the roof timbers were strong enough to carry a two-foot depth of snow. But in fact we never get more than a few inches up there before the wind blows between the merlons and drives it off."

"The tower has a nearly flat roof and has stood a long time," the Vicar said.

"I remember only once having to shovel snow from up there," agreed Plentey.

Lydia had come into the room and heard Adam Fry say, "I should like to see the view from the top of the tower."

Lydia joined in, "Joshua took me up last week. I loved watching the tiny people going about in the town. But I was surprised there was not a distant view. From the battlements at Middleham we could see such a long way." She turned to Woolman. "Father, may we bring in dinner?"

"Yes, Lyddie, thank you. Come to the table, friends."

Margery brought in the dishes and pots, helped by Tim, the young lad whose usual duties were to carry water from the well and wood for the fires, feed the dog and the fowls, help with the pigeons and run errands. Lydia hardly recognised him, wearing a new shirt and with his face scrubbed clean.

All the company stood around the table. Before the servants left the room, Richard asked, "Will you say Grace for us, Sir Geoffrey, please?"

"Benedic, Domine Deus, his donis, quae nobis ex liberalitate tua hodie dedisti; per Jesum Christum Dominum Nostrum. Amen."

Chapter 6
A VISIT TO MRS PLENTEY

John Plentey started his work as usual in his counting house one morning, before going out to meet a business friend at the Red Lion. He opened his door and found Lydia there about to knock.

"Come in, Lydia," he said, "I have to go out but my wife is here and will be pleased to see you."

Mrs Plentey heard him and hurried to greet Lydia. "Come in, Lydia, welcome. I have been so looking forward to seeing you."

"Thank you Mrs Plentey. I am sorry to hear you have not been well."

"I'm very much better, thank you. Come to the light now... yes, you resemble your father and I can see a likeness to your mother too."

Surprised by this Lydia said, "Oh do you remember her? I remember so little; just her being there and wanting to be with her. But I can't see her face."

"It was a sweet face. We knew each other as children. Then she went into the Countess of Warwick's service, before she was married you know, the countess I mean. We got to know each other again when she was newly wed. We all grieved with you and your father, Lydia. It was hard to lose such a sweet lady. Now, when you've told me your news I'll show you my garden. How is your father?"

"He's well, thank you."

"And have you heard from your friends at Middleham? And do you know the king and his family?"

Amused by the torrent of questions Lydia asked one too. "You are interested in the royal family?"

"Oh yes, I have a book with all their pictures... my sister sends them from London."

"Well, I saw the king once, but not to speak to. I know his young brother a little, Richard of Gloucester, as he was among the lads my lord was training at Middleham. We girls were kept away from them most of the time!"

"And did you see Queen Elizabeth? She is said to be very beautiful."

"Only from a distance. But one of her ladies brought the queen's little daughter, Princess Elizabeth, to play in the nursery. Isabel, Anne and I kept her amused for an hour. The earl is her godfather and often asks to see her."

"And what of George of Clarence? He is heir to the throne, is he not?"

"Yes, until the queen bears a son. I expect you have heard that he has just been married to my dear Isabel Neville."

"Oh yes. It was last week wasn't it? Where were they married?"

"In Calais. I had a letter today from Anne. She writes a good description of the wedding."

"She's the younger one, isn't she?" Mrs Plentey broke off as sounds reached them of two male voices in argument. "Here come the boys. Arguing as usual. Do sisters argue, Lydia, as brothers do?"

Laughing, Lydia replied, "Oh yes! Sometimes I found myself defending Anne against Isabel, who could be quite fierce. But it usually ended in laughter. We laughed so much, it hurt!"

Two young men erupted into the room. "Hullo Mother!" one of them said, "I didn't know thou hadst company."

"This is Lydia Woolman," his mother replied. "My son, Robert, Lydia. And this is Hugh." The young men bowed politely to Lydia.

"Lydia has recently come from Middleham Castle where she lived with my Lord of Warwick's family," Mrs Plentey continued.

"Then you can tell us what Warwick is really like," Hugh said. "I am an admirer but Robert says the earl is greedy for power."

"He is a brave man and the most kind and generous I have known."

"There you are then, Bob!"

Lydia continued, "But I am a little angry with him today as he is using his daughter's marriage in the political struggle just as any other great lord might."

"Not such a saint then, Hugh," Robert said. "He's as bad as any of them."

They seemed genuinely interested in Lydia's remarks so she kept on. "I have had much kindness from my lord, and the countess has been like a mother to me. The two girls are my dearest friends."

"And what is your opinion of Warwick's rebellion against the king?" asked Robert. "The wool trade is threatened you know, with the country in turmoil. Suppose he conquers King Edward in battle, what then? England can't flourish with two kings unable to rule!"

Lydia looked taken aback but laughed as Mrs Plentey said, "Now Robert, whyever should Lydia have to answer such a question?" Then they all laughed and the tension was broken.

Robert tried another tack. "How do you like Northleach, Lydia? May we take you to see our friends? I have to ride round the farms next week, would you like to come?"

"Thank you, but my father is keeping me busy in the counting house. Perhaps there'll be time later on."

Hugh took a turn. "I have to leave soon, with the next wool train. My father wants me to learn the business in Calais. Tell Mr Woolman I'll come round and see him before I go. I expect he may have letters for London and Calais."

"Thank you Hugh, I will remind him." Lydia didn't want to go on being the centre of so much attention and said, "I must be going, Mrs Plentey. May I see the garden next time?"

"Of course my dear." Mrs Plentey was already looking forward to having Lydia to herself on her next visit. "Goodbye, come again soon."

Lydia thanked her hostess for her kindness and was escorted to the door by the brothers, assuring them she could get safely home on her own.

Chapter 7
THE CHURCH OF SAINT PETER AND SAINT PAUL

In summer, working days for labourers were long, hot and exhausting. Cuthbert and Jack had been at the beck and call of Tom and of several masons all day in Northleach Church. They were supposed to be dismantling the scaffolding in the nave. Sturdy poles, roped together, had stood for years while the stonework was being completed. Tom had been reluctant to take it down while there was any possibility of alterations being needed. Now it had become his priority.

Jack had decided he was coming down for a bit of a break and reckoned he could jump the last six feet. Cuthbert was a little higher up and realised suddenly what was happening. If Jack did jump he would land on an unstable pile of poles and rubbish.

"Hey Jack!" he shouted. "Why go that way? What's the goddam ladder for?"

"Thought it would be quicker," Jack said, but he was a bit worried now, dangling, fast losing the strength to pull himself up again.

"Hang on!" Cuthbert shouted, as he nipped down the ladder. "Now jump! I can break yer fall."

He got his feet planted firmly and grabbed at Jack's shirt as he fell almost on top of him. "What devil's got into you, then?"

"Thanks mate," Jack gasped. "I don't know when I've been so stretched out."

"Ye should try King Edward's new torture then. It's the latest thing in London. It's a thundering rack

Northleach Church in 2014, eve dunlop Photography

with screws."

Cuthbert gave Jack a demonstration, flinging himself on to a pile of poles and stretching out.

"The feller ties yer hands and feet, then turns the blasting screw in the middle. Winds ye up till yer stretched fit to burst! That's after ye've had yer feet burned!"

Jack didn't seem all that impressed. "What's the point?" was all he said.

Cuthbert got to his feet. "Yer supposed to tell all ye know. If ye don't faint first. Be careful ye ain't charged with farting treason!"

Jack thought he could hear Tom coming. "We're supposed to finish these poles today. We'll have Tom after us."

Cuthbert scrambled back up the ladder. "You stay on the blasting floor. Catch what I drop. Ready?"

They appeared to be working quite effectively when Tom appeared. "Not finished yet? What's keeping you fellows? Ye'll have to work tonight till the whole lot's down. And I want you back first thing tomorrow to get all these poles stacked up outside. I've got the churchwardens coming at nine o'clock to talk about the floor paving."

Jack looked aggrieved. "We're working as fast as anyone could, Tom."

"You've never seen real work, my lad." Tom was tired. His ankle was playing up. But he'd need to be on the spot till the lads finished. He saw John Plentey come into the church and made a big effort to seem pleased. Standing talking was more tiring than anything else.

Plentey greeted Tom, then told him, "I think I've found just the man to make the Brass in memory of my father. I've seen some of his work and I like it. But he's a Londoner and I doubt he's ever seen a sheep in his life!"

"It's one thing to find the craftsman, sir, but I don't know where 'e'll get the latten for it. I've seen none since the troubles began."

"Leave that to me, Tom. I've a man going over to the Low Countries soon who can make enquiries. When you've a few minutes with nothing else to do, - ha, ha - Tom, I'd like to discuss with you where the brass is to go."

"Come and see me when we start the paving, sir."

"The design will show Father and Mother and their three children, and sheep of course, and the family woolmark."

"That'll look very fine, Mr Plentey."

"It's not to earn praise, Tom, but that their souls shall be remembered."

They both jumped at the sound of a loud crash. It sounded like planks falling. Tom turned, saying, "I must go and see what those lads are doing."

The Vicar started work on his notes for the St Peter and Paul festival service. Each year he meditated on these two towering figures of the New Testament. It had been his custom over the last few years to concentrate on either Peter or Paul and find something fresh to say each time. This year he decided to go back to the origin of Peter's ministry.

He opened his Bible at the story near the end of St John's Gospel. Jesus asked Peter, 'Simon Peter, do you love me?'

'Master, you know that I love you,' Peter had replied.

Jesus' next words were, 'Feed my sheep.'

It seemed that Peter was a little hurt that Jesus asked him the question three times. But to Geoffrey it seemed to be an echo of Peter's denial of Jesus three times over. Was he being forgiven three times?

Geoffrey would enlarge on the theme of the shepherd and the sheep as he had done many times before.

The sheep trust the shepherd. All pastors had a call to lead the sheep to nourishment as he was trying to do. His was a big responsibility, making the best translation he could from Latin to English of a parable of Jesus or one of the incidents from the gospels and conveying it as vividly as possible to his congregation. But the Latin text was sacred; he had to judge which parts it was wise to give to the common people.

Many were as familiar from childhood, as Peter would have been, with the words from ancient scripture, 'The Lord is my Shepherd'.

By the twenty-sixth of June traders and merrymakers were pouring into Northleach for the biggest fair of the year. It was now St Peter's Tide, Paul's too.

Simon hired an extra man to help make bread. Ellen had a friend round to bake pies with her and on hearing this, Lydia asked if she could help too. Bales of cloth were brought in from the Low Countries, woven from Northleach wool. With them came canvas and thread, lace and ribbons. Paper of various kinds came too; there were no papermakers in England. It was expensive but one could sometimes find a bargain price for a large packet which could be shared between friends.

Tom organised a great tidying-up of the church so that visitors might see it. The craftsmen and labourers were given three days off, provided each took a turn at watching all the valuable objects inside the church.

The weather stayed fine. Lydia found she was quite excited at the thought of Northleach's special occasion. As well as helping Ellen she had to prepare food for the house with Margery and make a bed ready for Adam Fry.

She was up early on the first day of the fair. Her father was occupied in the counting house discussing business with his cousin; Tim had been given the day off; Margery seemed to be well in control in the kitchen. Lydia went across to the bakery where Ellen was already doing a brisk trade in pies.

When everything was sold, the two girls prepared to make a round of the stalls. Ellen took charge and tied a big pouch round her waist where she could carry their purchases. She showed Lydia the best way to hide her purse in the front of her gown. They pushed through a crowd in the market place to watch two acrobats, and farther along came to an improvised bowling alley where Tim was competing with his friends. Lydia looked at the big display of prizes and wondered what would happen if Tim won the pig. Ellen bought some cloth and ribbons to make pretty things for her small god-daughter. Lydia found a little book of riddles and jokes and bought it for her father.

A band was playing loudly outside the Plenteys' house and Lydia saw Mr Plentey come out, hands over ears, and hurry off in the direction of the church.

At dinner time they returned to their homes agreeing to meet again in the cool of the evening.

Chapter 8
THE KING IMPRISONED

The summer days passed. Lydia had settled into a routine, helping Ellen with her reading, Margery with the housekeeping, her father with his figures. Sometimes there was a quiet hour in the afternoon when she might sit under the tree in the garden or roam the country around Northleach.

Lydia sorely missed Isabel and Anne but often thought how much more fortunate she was than they were. Anne, often lonely, not happy with the bustle of Calais, missing her rides on the moor above Middleham; Isabel, having to fit in with the demands of her father or of the Court and always on the move. Whenever her Cousin Fry or another reliable messenger was in Northleach, Lydia sent letters to London and Calais and occasionally one would come to her.

There were rumours of more trouble between Warwick and the king but most people had lost interest.

One day a letter came from Anne inviting Lydia to Warwick Castle. Anne and her mother had come over from Calais to London, but it was very hot there and they planned to spend a week at Warwick and were hoping Isabel might join them. The earl had given Anne permission to invite her friend. 'I'm so longing to see thee, Lyddie,' Anne wrote. Lydia's father was sympathetic but said that Joshua could not be spared to go with her.

Joshua saw how desperately Lydia wanted to go and told her that one of the shepherds had a sister living in Warwick; she implored her father to ask this man to accompany her. At last it was all arranged. Lydia was to spend one night with her friends while Stephen the shepherd would stay at his sister's. As the weather was so warm they would change horses at one of the inns, picking up their own mounts on the return journey. The inn at Halford had a good reputation and they would try there. They should make good speed.

As Lydia made her last minute preparations one of Fry's men clattered into the market place with shocking news. When Ellen called with a loaf in the morning she found to her surprise that Lydia was still at home and not on the Warwick road.

"As thou sees', I'm still here," Lydia said. "We heard yesterday that there has been a battle at Edgecote, near Banbury, and my Lord of Warwick has captured King Edward and holds him prisoner in Warwick Castle. Father decided I could not go."

"And thou so wanted'st to see Isabel and Anne."

"Yes, I've been looking forward to it so much."

"How can a baron like Warwick just take charge of the king? He can't be king himself."

"I fear he's made a big mistake. I reckon the king feels quite safe at Warwick Castle. He didn't have enough men about him to defy the earl. But now so many people will be outraged by what my lord has done, support for the king will grow."

"So the people have some power after all," mused Ellen. "They will not stand for two kings being in prison. What a difficult position this puts poor Isabel in."

"Yes, I've been thinking about that too. The countess and Anne must still be in London and probably Isabel too. And it's difficult to see how King Edward could ever forgive Warwick again."

Ellen left to get back to her work. Lydia found her father on the doorstep checking a list.

"Thread for the woolpacks, wine for the guests, a

shopping list for Mrs Plentey's sister, feed for the horses, ask Joshua about another pigeon... *Timothy!*" He was making his usual preparations for the departure of a wool train. She knew better than to interrupt.

Tim came hurtling through the yard in answer to the call. "Mr Woolman, sir."

"Tim, hast thou counted the woolpacks going on Thursday?"

"Yes sir, twenty sarplers going altogether."

"Are there enough horses?"

"We need one more sir, I was just going round to the King's Head."

"Hm... All right, lad, try the King's Head. And go round to barber Gregory. I need my hair cut today! Fix a time for me."

Later, Richard discussed matters with Simon. He had just heard that Warwick had seized the queen's father, Lord Rivers, and her elder brother, Sir John Woodville. They had been executed without trial.

"This will cost Warwick the sympathy of many of his supporters," Simon said. "More people will suddenly rally to the king and queen."

Besides this, the two friends agreed that armies taking action near Banbury were much too close for comfort. They recalled the time, when their daughters were young children, when news had come of the Battle of St Albans. King Harry had sat in the market place while soldiers poured through narrow lanes and over garden walls. There was terrible loss of life but also havoc for the local citizens and their property. The struggle which was so important to the factions of York and Lancaster seemed interminable to ordinary folk who wished above all that the strife could be concluded.

Next day King Edward was moved to Middleham Castle where he was more remote from London and fewer men were likely to question Warwick's judgment. Lydia thought of him making the long journey she had made. She wondered if he was in one of the dungeons or perhaps more comfortably housed in the family's apartment. The old nursery had barred windows to keep children safe.

Things were turning out as she had guessed. Warwick had no power without the king. No soldiers would obey his commands without a signature from King Edward. It was not long before Warwick had to back down and set his captive free. Men with all kinds of grievances had turned out to fight for him but would not follow him in defying the king. The uncertainty led to general lawlessness. While Warwick was trying to establish order, the king, joined by his close affinity, was able to march into York. From there he returned to London.

Lydia and her father were shaken by Warwick's ruthless action against the queen's family. Lydia could not reconcile it with her knowledge of his generous spirit and gentleness with his family and friends. Certainly, the Woodvilles had made themselves unpopular in many quarters; they seemed to have undue influence over the king, they expected Queen Elizabeth to put them forward for positions of power that others were entitled to, and the queen's sisters were snapping up the most eligible bridegrooms. Lydia smiled ruefully as she remembered how Isabel had said after each of the betrothals, "We must celebrate another happy release!" She knew her father had a list of possible husbands for her.

A boy from Yanworth brought Geoffrey Langbroke a letter from the Vicar there. A woman with five young children had been turned out of a farm cottage. Her husband had been caught stealing a pig, tried and sent to Gloucester gaol. The farmer had hired a new labourer at Stow Fair in May and needed the cottage for him and his family. The neighbours had done their best but there was no-one who could take the whole family in and winter would soon be here. It seemed to Geoffrey that Northleach, with its greater resources, should be able to provide help. He consulted Simon Trencher and they agreed to speak to John Plentey. Plentey owned the two tumbledown cottages at Mill End that had been abandoned since the last flooding two or three years earlier. This is where the Hampnett Brook, which runs along the main street and the lower side of the market place, flows into the River Leach. The brook, usually quiet, is occasionally swollen by the higher springs that run only after a few days of exceptional rainfall.

The lower cottage had been left to fall down and had had several stones removed, under cover of darkness, for repairs elsewhere. The upper cottage had not been damaged so much by floodwater and was sometimes used as shelter by vagrants stopping on a journey.

John Plentey agreed that the homeless family might be housed there for the winter and sent a man round to check the roof and replace a few missing tiles. The churchwardens organized a party of young men to chop wood and make big fires for three days before the family's arrival. A cart was sent over to Yanworth to fetch them. Ellen and Lydia took candles, a big pot of soup and two loaves and made sure all the children were fed before nightfall, while their mother arranged their bedding and her few belongings. She said she was willing to knit and spin to earn a few pennies to buy bread and vegetables, but Ellen realised she could not possibly earn enough to feed them all.

In the next few days Ellen asked several of her friends and neighbours for help. They decided to find as many people as they could who would each give a little help, so that their combined efforts could make all the difference. One woman went round all the cottagers who kept fowls and asked for two eggs from each till she had made up a dozen. Many agreed to do this every week. When a pig was killed, a joint of its meat could always be spared for the needy family. Woolman told Trencher he would pay for two loaves for the family every day. And so they could be sustained through the winter until the young man was due for release from prison.

Chapter 9
FACING THE WINTER

Autumn came with King Edward safely back on his throne, certain he could ride out the storm.

In the church, work progressed smoothly. The paving was started and Mr Plentey's brass was set in the floor. When the frosts began, work came to a standstill. Men with cold fingers can carve neither stone nor wood. They found what work they could about the town but those who had put no money by had some hungry days. Tom was glad enough to have a break and had always saved a little to see himself through the hard times. He suffered a good deal though. His aches and pains were bad when it rained and he was liable to get a chesty cough. His neighbours made sure he always had a good fire.

The younger men were glad to earn a few pence where they could, fetching water or chopping firewood for widowed housewives. The women and children passed the darker hours knitting or spinning. Many of the men knitted too and gave the women long strips to sew together by daylight to make a blanket or shawl. Many Northleach people depended on knitted garments or on the rough cloth woven in Northleach or Cirencester from homespun wool.

A sheepskin coat was made for the Vicar for his morning prayers in the cold church. He had good health and never missed a day.

Lydia found the house cold, away from the living-room and kitchen fires. She disliked going up the garden to the privy, particularly in darkness and rain. Everyone around her was accustomed to that and thought nothing of it.

She missed her friends more now. At Middleham the winter had passed so comfortably with plenty of servants to stoke up the fires, frequent guests and parties and feasts, and games and competitions dreamed up by Isabel and Anne. At Christmas they had always devised a play to perform to the grown-ups and spent hours making and adjusting their costumes.

The young people in Northleach invited Lydia to their celebrations at Christmas and her father did his best to make it a festive time. She felt ashamed to be comparing their efforts with the grand functions at Middleham.

In the flat days at the end of the year Lydia's spirits were lifted when a letter arrived from Anne. She took it at once to show to Ellen. Not sure how her friend would find Anne's handwriting, she read it aloud to her:

"Darling Lyddie,

We're all here now together, at Warwick, and Father says I may invite thee over as soon as the spring weather comes. Isabel says that she and George hope to go for a while to our house at Burford and that would be easier for thee.

We all went to Westminster for Christmas. I was surprised the king wanted us after all the things that happened last summer. Queen Elizabeth was not at all pleased and hardly spoke to us. Well, I wouldn't, if my guest had just beheaded my father and brother. The king seems determined it should look to the people as if he and Father agree. If I were Father I would be glad to be given a second chance. But I'm not and you know Father!

What I want most is to get back to Middleham - though it wouldn't be the same without thee, Lyddie. Isabel sends her love and says she will write soon. Did she tell thee she is pregnant? The baby is due in April. It had better be a boy to cheer up Father. She is keeping well. I enclose a picture of Westminster Palace in winter. I hope thou likest it.

A thousand kisses from Anne."

The two girls discussed this letter in detail. It brought her friends so vividly to Lydia's mind that her mood lifted from that day. Surely everything would go well now. The earl would feel no need to upset the king again. The countess would be busy with preparations for the grandchild.

Lydia would ask her father if she and Ellen could hold a party here and she would invite all the folk who had been kind to her.

Chapter 10
THE MARCH TO THE COAST

The snow came one night early in the new year. In the morning, Lydia put on several layers of woollen garments and took the old dog up the hill behind the house. The wind had dropped and everything was quiet. The sun shone weakly through grey clouds but gave its brightness to blue sky overhead and to the north-west skyline where the trees stood out bravely. She continued up the hill north-eastward, where the ground could barely be distinguished from the sky, one white lying against the other like a ewe's fleece beside a lamb's.

She came to a great ash tree; snow lay on every branch but had already dripped from the twigs. It stood out against a distant copse, silver with snow and shaded with grey. The dog made the only strong contrast, dark against the snow with its shadow very soft in the weak sunlight.

She turned to look back south-westward. A mist had blotted out part of the valley, veiling the shapes of the town, only the church tower clearly defined. Before she was home, the mist had rolled away, the sun had cleared the clouds, the shadows had sharpened and the snow began to drip from the roofs.

Spring came at last. It was still cold but the days lengthened and Lydia went out every day to see the first of the newborn lambs. The news from London was grim. There were rebellions against King Edward in the North and it was found that the Earl of Warwick was involved. The Duke of Clarence's loyalty to his father-in-law was strained to the uttermost. No word came from Isabel but Lydia thought of her constantly and agonised over her situation.

One morning at the beginning of April, Ellen was in her place in her father's shop, her usual customers coming in for their loaves. She was startled by a clatter of horses' hooves outside and suddenly two soldiers burst in, dressed in King Edward's livery. One man strode up to the counter and said, "Madam, the king has need of all your bread. I am commanded to pay you the full amount. And that's for your trouble." He had a coin in one hand and a small money bag in the other and gave them to Ellen. "Put it all in the sack, Dan." He held one corner of the sack and Dan held the other and quickly scooped up all the loaves from the counter and dropped them in. He glanced round the shop.

Ellen said, "Thank you sir, but all the loaves on this shelf are ordered by the people of the town who will call shortly."

Dan promptly took those too and his officer continued, "Then tell the baker from the king, he'll need to start baking again at once."

Ellen opened her mouth to speak but no words came. The men and the bread had disappeared in a flash. Her father came in to tell her that the oven was now ready if anyone brought in a pie to be cooked, then saw the empty counter. "The bread! Thou canst not have sold it already."

"The king's men have taken it all," she said. "The fellow said thou'd need to start baking all over again." She was flushed and indignant.

"I heard nothing."

"Thou wert stoking the fire."

The door opened again and Lydia came in. "Ellen! Tim says there's no bread to be had."

"That's so. I've heard of the king's army helping themselves but I never thought of it happening to us."

Trencher gave Lydia a wry smile. "Well, I'd better start again. Thou canst accept pies for baking for the next hour, my dear, while the dough's rising."

Of course, everyone had seen the soldiers. Ellen and Lydia were questioned by their neighbours and it took Lydia some time to make her way home through the market place.

It seemed that even the work at the church was affected. Tom was finding it more difficult than usual to keep an eye on his labourers.

"Cuthbert! Jack!" he called out in the nave. Then he spotted Jack at the far end of the south aisle but what he could be doing there was a mystery. "There you are, Jack. There's work to be done, ye know. Where's Cuthbert?"

"Dunno, Tom. Maybe up on the roof. Joshua's up there, he p'raps wanted something taken up. I'll go and see." He ambled off on his imaginary errand. Before Tom could comment, Cuthbert came in through the door at the foot of the tower.

"There you are, lad. Did I see you taking the cart out to the main road?" Tom didn't miss much.

"Yes, Tom, I thought I'd shift some o' that blasting rubble, while it's not raining."

"That'll keep for another day. Today you're to clear up the whole of this floor in the nave, like I told you first thing this morning. Get all these waste ends of wood into a heap down there and next time it rains ye can chop it fer kindling. While it's fine get everything else out of here and stack up anything that can be used."

"Right away, Tom." Cuthbert knew it was time he proved his usefulness.

Jack appeared, taking care not to be intercepted by Tom. "I've been up on the roof, looking for 'ee."

Cuthbert straightened up and leant on the broom. "Well, son, with my keen ears I thought I could hear carts rumbling and men shouting so I took a load of farting rubble out to the Fosse where it'll be needed for filling potholes sooner or later. There's an army of twenty thousand marching to Cirencester!"

"The king's army? I saw some fellows in the market place. Thought they was wearing king's colours."

"Right. I walked up the hill alongside one of their ruddy baggage wagons. Fellow told me they left Nottingham twelve days ago. The lads on foot have no puff fer talking. They're chasing after the Earl of Warwick. Think 'e's going to Exeter for a ship. 'E's been charged wi' treason."

"'Ow many miles they walk each day then?"

"About fifteen. They camped near Bourton last night. Hope to get to Cirencester this evening. I walked down again to pick up the goddam cart, gave a boy a farthing to mind it; might have been thundering requisitioned! There was a column of men and wagons as far as the eye could see."

It would soon be Easter time. The Vicar looked around the church. Perhaps the nave could be tidied up sufficiently for the Easter Day Service. There was no scaffolding now, but a substantial barrier between the south aisle and the nave kept people away from the masons' benches. He could ask for volunteers to clean the east window and, though the nave seemed bare without the screen, he could perhaps preach from the chancel steps. When he put this to Tom he saw how difficult Tom found it, wanting to please him but needing the work to go ahead without interruption. Geoffrey knew he must overcome the impatience he felt. He was chastened by the thought of all the men who had gone before him who had had the vision to embark on the improvements, knowing they would never see them completed.

Over the next week he re-read the Easter story carefully. Jesus had preached in local synagogues and made a special journey to the temple in Jerusalem. But the buildings were not important to him in themselves. His mission was to carry out the will of his Father and reach out to all the people.

Geoffrey tried to think out the real purpose of the church they were rebuilding. All the townspeople were united in the common goal of making it as fine as it could be. It was a symbol of the community he served. But when he proclaimed on Easter Day, 'Christ is risen', it didn't matter where he stood.

Chapter 11
ISABEL'S BABY

Towards the end of April, with the lambs growing almost visibly into their ill-fitting fleeces, Lydia was out on one of her accustomed walks when, in a bend in the path, she suddenly came across a young man walking towards her.

"Hugh! I didn't expect to see you here."

"Hullo, Lydia. I'm only just home from Calais. I've come up here for a lungful of good clean air; London stinks."

"Is there any news from Calais? I've heard nothing from the Neville girls."

"Oh Lydia, did you not know about Isabel Neville giving birth aboard ship?"

"No! Have they come safely to land?"

"Isabel is well. They went ashore in Normandy. The baby died." Impulsively he took Lydia's hand, for the news distressed her. "It was a boy. My Lord of Warwick is sorely grieved. The people talk of it as an ill omen."

Lydia freed her hand and crossed herself. "May he rest in peace. Poor little mite." She became very quiet. Then she said, "How soon did they come into land?"

"The king had ordered the port of Calais to be closed to the Earl of Warwick. You know he had charged him with treason?"

"Yes, we heard that."

"The sea had been rough but other ships were docking as usual. My lord had to continue down the Channel."

"But no more news?"

"No, nothing reliable," Hugh said. "London is alive with rumours of course. Warwick has landed in this port or that... he might persuade King Louis to raise troops for him... or Warwick might join forces with Queen Marguerite." Hugh said that to lighten the mood and Lydia laughed; it was the most unlikely thing in the world.

They began to walk together in the direction Lydia had been taking.

"What are your plans, Hugh? Will you soon be travelling again?"

"My father wants me here for the wool-packing. Now I'm in such good time I expect I'll be out with the shepherds checking the ewes and lambs. May I walk with you, Lydia?"

"Thanks, Hugh. I must be getting back."

"You must tell me what's been going on here while I've been away."

Lydia found herself chattering comfortably with Hugh. She told him about the soldiers taking the bread, the time it had taken for the army on the Fosseway to march by, the kindness she had received from Hugh's mother.

Hugh asked her about her life with the Neville family and told her he had lived a few weeks at his uncle's in London before he first went to Calais. The Warwick family home was in the same part of the City. The earl was famous for his generosity; hungry people coming to the kitchen door were never turned away. Lydia agreed he had a truly generous spirit. Isabel had told her her father could be fierce or stubborn, sometimes both at once, but she had always found him kindly. He had made her feel included as one of his girls. And so they arrived at their homes, not far apart across the market place.

Suddenly alone, Lydia felt a great tide of sorrow for Isabel and went in to share the news with her father.

The young man who had stolen the pig was released from Gloucester gaol before Stow Fair in May. There he was hired by a farmer from Condicote. The churchwardens paid a carter to take the family to their new home. Ellen and Lydia went round to help them pack up their things and to say goodbye to the woman and children they had come to know well. John Plentey was mightily relieved that the river hadn't risen in the winter and that the family had been kept safe and well while in Northleach.

It was nearly a month later when Lydia went out to the yard one day and found her father coming towards the house holding a tiny fragment of paper.

He said, "The pigeon has come from Calais at last, but I can make neither head nor tail of this message. It seems to be just a list of numbers."

"May I see it?"

Richard handed her the paper. "I was hoping it was from Adam's man in Calais telling me the price the wool is fetching."

"It's from Isabel Neville, Father! It must be for me."

Her father snatched the paper back. "How dost thou know that?"

"It's in the code we made up as children. Anyway, it's Isabel's handwriting. I'd know those sevens anywhere."

He handed the paper back to her. "Then it must be for thee. But it's annoying. Polly is the fastest pigeon I've ever had and I told Adam to keep her for the most important news."

"Then I'll decode it right away," Lydia said.

They went into the house. Lydia went to a cupboard and took out her box. She opened it and found the code book Isabel had given her. She began to scribble on a piece of paper.

Tim knocked on the door and came in to see

Woolman.

"What is it, Tim?"

"The wool-packers have arrived already, sir. They got as far as Minster Lovell last night. I saw them go into the King's Head."

"Good lad. Go round there and say I'll be ready to see them in about an hour."

When Tim had gone, Lydia said, "I think I can make some sense of this, Father. It seems to be an important message from my Lord of Warwick." But Woolman was by now preoccupied with wool business. "Father, I think this is important."

"Important message! It's just a game with a string of numbers. Warwick has never sent me an important message. Except... the one telling me my daughter was coming home." He smiled. "Come on, how does this confounded code work?"

"It's a secret. I can't tell thee. Only we three girls understand it. I can only say that the numbers relate to a story we made up. We were sure there were sentences in it that would cover anything that could possibly happen. There are only three copies of the book."

"May I see it?"

Lydia handed him the book and he flicked through it. He said rather scornfully, "This is just a story for children; how can it cover everything?"

"Shall I read thee the message?"

"Yes, yes, what is it?" he said impatiently.

Lydia read from her notes, "Let him know my plans. Who? The Captain of Warwick Castle. My headquarters is at a town beginning with V. Near a port beginning with B. Across the sea. More than a hundred miles south of Winchester."

Richard still wasn't impressed. He said, "I'm a bit lost."

"It needs sorting out a bit. Give me a moment." After writing a bit more, she tried again. "Is this clearer? Inform the Captain of Warwick Castle, my headquarters is at... (we must look at a map). It means a place in Normandy. Send me reports from... (which are the important towns in the north? Durham and Carlisle?) I need birds to fly from France to the Midlands (that's to us, here,) as a staging post for messengers to the north of England. The password is BEEHIVE. Hast thou a map, Father?"

At last she had his full attention. Richard went to a chest and rummaged in it and eventually brought out a rolled map. "Here's a map of England with a little bit of the French coast." He spread it out on the table.

"Winchester is marked. Due south is this bit of Normandy. There's a place on the coast called Barfleur. Dost think that's it?"

"I can't see anything else beginning with B. I must send word to my lord's men at Warwick Castle. They will have maps of the French lands there. I shall have to let them have all the pigeons that are in good condition to go to Normandy. I must write a message for my lord. Wilt thou translate it into code?"

"Yes, of course, Father. Dost thou think my lord really has a plan that will work?"

"We don't know all the circumstances... but I think Warwick is in a desperate situation. If anyone can find a way out, he will. And I will do anything I can to help." He sat down at his desk and started to write.

Tim was soon back from the King's Head. Before he could speak, Richard said to him, "Find Joshua and tell him I need him at once."

Later that day, Lydia thought about the time when she and Isabel had made up the story that formed the basis of the code book. Isabel had insisted that they must think of everything that could possibly happen and every word or phrase that might be needed. When the story was finished, each word or short phrase was given a number. When a number appeared in the text it was to be written in brackets to avoid confusion. They had long discussions about whether one number could cover 'on' and 'in', or perhaps 'to' and 'for'. Anne joined in and invented funny sentences where the whole meaning was changed by whether it was 'on' or 'in' until they all dissolved into giggles.

At the end of the message the pigeon had brought, were the numbers 144, 145, which Lydia remembered without having to look them up: 'Be careful, there are seasoned spies about.' She had been startled at the time with the seriousness Isabel showed, insisting this was important.

Chapter 12
RUPERT THE MASON

June came. May blossom gave way to elderflower and dog-rose. At noon, the ewes, newly-shorn, gathered under the ash trees, in full-leaf now, giving deep shade.

Woolman's old dog lay stretched out on his side in the sun, till he got too hot and moved, panting, into the shade near the house. At the church, the sweating labourers paused frequently to drink the water they had brought up from the river in two large pitchers early in the morning.

Tom and Joshua were deep in discussion, Tom with one eye on the labourers. The door from the porch opened and a man of about forty-five came in and strode confidently across to Tom.

"Hullo there, Tom! It's been a long time!"

For a few seconds Tom was nonplussed. But he knew that voice. He said, "Rupert! It's good to see you, lad."

"There's no work going on at Windsor just now, so I thought I'd travel a bit through the summer and autumn and pick up work where I can."

"I can certainly find work for you here," Tom said warmly. He could hardly believe his luck.

"Joshua, this is Rupert who served his apprenticeship here and went on to become a master mason. He works for the king. He's one of Northleach's successes, ye know."

"Glad to meet you, sir," Joshua said.

"And you, Joshua."

"Joshua is my right hand, Rupert, he's me legs

too; goes up ladders to see what's what, now that I'm that bit older."

"You look hardly a day older to me, Tom." Rupert smiled at him. "Tell me how the church work is going."

"Come in to the nave. Old Mr Plentey's dream has come true, ye see."

"This is very fine work! I'd like the boys at Windsor to see this!" Rupert walked up and down gazing up at the columns and windows, Tom and Joshua at his side, answering his questions.

Jack and Cuthbert quietly left the church by the porch door. It was standing open; the click of the latch could have given them away. For once, Tom did not notice.

Rupert said, "I started here nearly thirty years ago, Joshua, so I can remember the old nave. I had a hand in the demolition myself. And you've seen every stage, Tom. It's your life's work, isn't it? You should have a memorial brass!"

"Tom's taught me all I know," Joshua told him.

"Well, now we've all praised each other, tell me what's still to do?"

"There's carving to be done. We need a figure for the niche outside on the gable of the nave. St John Baptist."

"And the pulpit, Tom," said Joshua.

"Yes, you'd be just the man to carve a new pulpit, Rupert. I'll look out the drawing - but I think I can give you a free hand with the detail."

"I can start tomorrow, Tom. I noticed as I came in, the porch is still unfinished."

"Yes. Now the nave's nearly done, the churchwardens have been discussing whether to finish the porch next. The plan was to improve the south aisle at the same time. But, of course, the porch is in constant use and the Vicar is still holding services in the south aisle. So we're to finish the north aisle next."

"And will you make an entrance into the north aisle for folks to use when later on the porch is full of scaffolding and workmen?"

"Yes, we've left one bay open while we're bringing in materials, to save damaging the porch. I'll get it screened for the winter and we'll build up the stonework next year and make a doorway then."

"I can stay the rest of the season, Tom, if you'll have me."

"That'll suit me well. Now tell me the news from Windsor."

They were startled by a loud crash and rumbling noise. Tom recalled there had been a cart loaded with rubble standing outside. He turned to Joshua.

"Run after those lads for me will you. They're nothing but trouble." When he had gone, Tom had a question for Rupert. "Would you say King Edward's secure now, Rupert? Now he's chased Warwick out of the country."

"I certainly hope so. It was a bad day when Warwick got away. I wouldn't write him off though, yet."

"That Edward's too soft-hearted. I expect 'e still wants 'is brother, Clarence, back. Probably mourns the loss of 'is cousin Warwick's friendship. Spared King Harry's life too. That's no way to show authority. Still, he's the best ruler we've had, in my lifetime."

"He'll do better yet. You'll see."

Chapter 13
SAINT PAUL'S EXAMPLE

Geoffrey Langbroke, the Vicar of Northleach, enjoyed the warm summer evenings. After a busy day of prayer, visiting and study, followed by a nourishing meal cooked by one of the women from the cottages near the church, he loved to sit for a while outside his house watching the water streaming to the mill and listening to the birds.

St Peter and St Paul's tide was coming round again. Geoffrey must soon decide on his subject for the festival service.

This year he would speak of Paul. Paul had experienced neither the earthly company of Jesus as Peter and James and John had, nor the revelations on the day of Pentecost.

His hearing of the risen Christ on the Damascus road had turned him from persecuting the early Christians to joining them. As his confidence grew he could hope to change the lives of the Gentiles.

This morning Geoffrey had looked up Paul's Epistle to the Galatians. Should he try to explain to his congregation that Paul had perceived a certain smugness among the Jews who had turned to Jesus. They still kept to many of the provisions of the Jewish law. They had been accustomed to looking down on the Pagans. Their forefathers had been the Chosen People. Paul was a Jew, so he should understand how they felt about Pagans who turned Christian.

But Paul told them again and again that there must be no superior and inferior followers of Jesus.

All were to be one in Christ.

On a visit to Paul and the Gentile Christians at Antioch, Peter had accepted them wholeheartedly. But when some of the other brothers arrived from Jerusalem, knowing that they still kept the rules of ritual washing, and sensitive to their opinion, Peter went back on his usual practice of eating with the Gentiles. He even reprimanded some of Paul's companions who did not follow the old ritual.

Paul rebuked Peter publicly and again preached his message: the new law of love was for all people, Jew and Greek, master and slave, male and female. The Christians must have no fear of seeming peculiar. A lesson as hard to learn today as it was then.

Peter, to his credit, recognised Paul's authority and accepted the rebuke. The rituals themselves were unimportant and obscured their original basis in common sense and cleanliness. The important thing was Jesus' message. The Jews must realise that the Gentiles were sensitive to the air of superiority sometimes worn by those who had been Christ's earthly companions.

Geoffrey found this incident deeply interesting but it was not likely to be understood by his uneducated people. He would do better to keep his message simple: God had promised Abraham, 'All nations will be blessed through you.' The brothers and sisters were to love each other as Jesus had loved them.

The light was fading and the air cooling. Geoffrey rose from his bench and went indoors for prayers and bed.

Chapter 14
NEWS FROM NORMANDY

On the 24th June a traveller rode into the town with letters. One was for Lydia. When she had read it she took it round to the Trenchers' house and found Ellen picking fruit in the garden.

"Ellen! I've heard from Isabel and Anne at last. I thought thou'd like to read the letters too. So much has happened to the girls."

Ellen was glad of an excuse for a break and took Lydia to the bench under the pear tree.

"Read them to me, Lydia, my hands are sticky."

"I think thou mightst have difficulty with the handwriting in any case, specially Isabel's. They're the first letters I've had since they left England in April. I'll start with Anne's, it's very short.

"Dear Lyddie,

I rode my darling pony all the way from Warwick Castle to Exeter and passed the end of thy road. I was so cross we couldn't stop to see thee but we had an army of twenty thousand chasing after us."

"The army that took our bread!"

"We were glad Isabel was already in Exeter. George had insisted the month before that she would be safer there and he was right. I am coming to see thee, Lyddie, as soon as we get back to England.

Love and kisses from Anne.

Now for Isabel's letter," Lydia continued. "Thou

remember'st the family took ship in Exeter? Warwick was expecting his usual welcome in Calais where he is so well-known." She spread the letter out on her knee.

"Darling Lydia,

Thank thee for thy letter. It took a month to get here. Thank thee for thy kind words about the baby. The grief was not as great as thou supposed because once I was safely ashore and felt well at last, I just thought nothing could ever be so terrible again. In a way, George is the more upset. He'd set his heart on having a son before the king did. Now he's heard from his sister that Queen Elizabeth is pregnant again.

Father is very restless; he so wanted a grandson. He was angry with the king when we were prevented from entering Calais and thinks the baby could have been saved. Mother said it was a very weak and small child and wouldn't have had much of a chance on dry land.

She was so good, Lyddie. She kept calm and managed to give me a bit of courage. She had her old servants Esther and Faith with her. The three of them have attended a great many births together. We had already been twelve days at sea when labour began and I had been seasick most of that time. I thought I was going to die; I have never felt so wretched.

We were warned not to enter the harbour at Calais. At first my father couldn't believe it and we anchored within range of their cannon fire. Father sent a message to his old friend, Lord Wenlock, but he had had orders from the king to keep us out.

He sent two casks of wine as a gift and warned us it was not safe to come in. I had a little wine as soon as I was able to swallow anything and it helped."

Lydia paused and saw the look of horror on Ellen's face.

"How could King Edward do that? Didn't he know about the baby?"

"He may not have known Isabel was near her time. Anyway, women's business doesn't really count when you've charged your old friend with treason." Lydia went on reading the letter.

"The sea was calmer when we sailed down the coast from Calais. Father was still in a furious mood. There were ships out looking for us and we were soon in the midst of battle. We captured some Burgundian ships and Father had the sailors thrown overboard. Our ships anchored off Honfleur on the first of May. It was so good to be ashore at last. Father asked for an audience of the French king but Louis was not at all pleased about the capture of the ships. He could not be seen to approve or he would be breaking the terms of his agreement with the Duke of Burgundy. At last, two days ago, King Louis sent for Father and George and received them at the Palace of Amboise. Mother, Anne and I had to stay here at Valognes. Queen Marguerite and her son Prince Edouard are not far away at Angers. I am quite curious to see what they are like."

Lydia stopped reading and said, "Now this part is written later.

14th June. Father and George have arrived

back and are sending a man to Calais
tomorrow with important messages. I
thought Father and King Louis were
supposed to be old friends but George says
they're like two dogs sniffing round each
other. Not growling so far. But even so,
King Louis gave them a good welcome and
so did Queen Charlotte. Her baby is
expected this month. Anne is here with
me. I enclose her note. My love to you.
Until we meet again, Isabel."

"How long has the letter taken?"

"Ten days. I feel so much better now, knowing
how things are for them." Lydia did not point out to
Ellen two numbers at the end of the letter: 144, 145.
The rest was not encoded, but then there was
nothing private in it.

A few days later Ellen and Lydia were once more
caught up in the excitement of St Peter's Fair.

Chapter 15
SIR GILBERT DE VILLEPION

On the last day of St Peter's Fair, Woolman made his usual evening round of the yard, checking his animals and birds. Lydia often heard him saying goodnight to the horses and making soothing sounds to the pigeons but this evening, midsummer dusk coming so late, she had gone up to bed.

All seemed peaceful and he started towards the house, when suddenly he became aware that he was not alone. The catch on the gate had made only the slightest click and the old dog had given only the softest growl. "Who's there?" he said.

A voice, hardly audible, said, "My Lord of Warwick sent me." A dark shape came towards Woolman. "Let me in quietly," the man said.

They went into the house and Woolman picked up the lamp from the table and held it up to see the intruder's face. Trying to sound calmer than he felt, he said, "How do I know you are from Warwick?"

The stranger took something from his pocket. "Here is the token you sent with Joshua to Warwick Castle."

Woolman set the lamp down on the table and took the small medallion from him and recognised it.

"You're right to be cautious," the visitor continued. "My name is Sir Gilbert de Villepion. My family has been in my lord's service for many years. Have you told anyone about Joshua's ride to Warwick Castle, apart from your daughter?"

"No." Woolman felt uneasy. He would have liked to

keep Lydia out of it. Sir Gilbert paced up and down the room, which unnerved him still more.

Then he said, "How did Joshua cover his strange disappearance?"

"He told his wife there were urgent orders from London for fells for the Whitsun markets. The wool train was about to leave. He was to ride round the small farms and the butchers."

"Fells?"

"A fell is a sheepskin with a good fleece on it. They have a scarcity value in the summer."

"Has he run errands like that for you before?"

"Yes."

"My Lord of Warwick needs a reliable man, centrally placed in England to receive his messages."

"I am only an ordinary man, sir, I doubt I can be much help to the earl."

"It is because you are unimportant that you can be useful to my lord." He resumed his pacing. Woolman still felt uneasy. He wasn't sure whether he would prefer to be unimportant or useful.

"How reliable are your pigeons?" Sir Gilbert continued.

"Young birds have been lost in training flights. I have sent only my best ones to Calais and Antwerp. There are always risks, but in two years, only one has failed to return." His pride in his birds gave him a new confidence.

"I think you'll do." The tone was chilly. "Have you ever lent money to King Edward?"

"No."

"Is business good?"

"Reasonably so. But these uncertain times make difficulties."

"I've been told to pay you well if I like the look of you."

Again Woolman had the churning feeling of a mixed reaction. He kept his voice steady. "Do you?"

"Yes. But you must take a solemn oath that you

will keep faith with my Lord of Warwick and not help his enemies. He has decided once and for all that Edward's foolishness has lost him the right to govern England. Do you agree?"

"King Edward has done me no harm. I regret my Lord of Warwick could not stay friends with him."

"My lord told me King Louis of France is ready to help him. King Louis has influence over Queen Marguerite. Prince Edouard is now of age and will play his part. My Lord of Warwick will guide him. What is it, Woolman?"

Woolman had indeed looked startled by this news. "Excuse me, sir, I had not heard that my lord is willing to back the Lancastrians."

"No, I don't suppose you hear much in a small place like this."

Woolman bristled. What could he say to make this man go away? His devotion to Warwick was being sorely tried. "I am in the wool trade, sir." After all he was *not* unimportant, was he? "King Edward has shown understanding of business. Most of our wool is sold in the Low Countries in the Duke of Burgundy's realm. I can't help being surprised that my Lord of Warwick is putting our trade at risk."

"You're questioning his judgment, Woolman?"

"No, sir, I can't see the whole picture as he can. Nothing will alter my loyalty to the earl."

"Now that my lord is promised help from France and with all King Henry's supporters in the West Country and Wales, and his own men, of course, he will have a much larger army than Edward of York. The Earl of Warwick will bring peace to the nations and trade will prosper. I'll return tomorrow, Woolman."

Sir Gilbert slipped out and Woolman bolted the back gate. He sat down at his table, his head in his hands. He felt drained of energy. The picture of Warwick working with his old enemy, King Harry's French wife, was utterly ludicrous. And what was

King Louis up to?

In the morning he wondered if Sir Gilbert's visit had been a bad dream. But the medallion was in his pocket.

Chapter 16
ANNE AND PRINCE EDOUARD

At the end of July the lambs were parted from the ewes. The sound of bleating was incessant and could only be escaped by folk who went indoors and shuttered the windows. Most people got used to it just before it suddenly stopped. One evening Richard Woolman and his friend, Simon Trencher, sat in Woolman's garden over a cup of ale. The bleating was so much part of their life it did not disturb them. After their usual discussion of local events they sat for a while in companionable silence. Simon knew his old friend almost too well.

"Out with it, Richard," he said. "I know thou hast something on thy mind."

Woolman was silent, wondering how much to say. At last he told him, "I think I've just started a new life as a spy and I'm not sure I like it."

"Whatever dost thou mean?"

"I should keep this to myself. I can trust thee, Simon, of course, but I didn't want to burden thee with it."

"It sometimes helps to talk things over."

"My Lord of Warwick found out about my homing pigeons. A pigeon from Calais brought a message - it must be two months ago – in a code that only Lydia and the two Neville girls understand. My lord needs my help."

"But now he stands charged with treason."

"Exactly." Richard paused, then said, "His latest message was to men in the North Country who are stirring up trouble to draw King Edward out of London."

"Is the earl about to return to England?"

"He intends to come before the autumn gales. King Louis has promised ships and men for an invasion of England."

"It'll be getting late in the season."

"The longer it's put off the better will King Edward be prepared," Richard said. They were silent for a little; the sound of bleating suddenly seemed louder.

"So Lydia is the only person in England who could understand Warwick's message and this pigeon was the only bird that could bring it to her."

Richard smiled agreement. He heard voices at the gate. He rose as Fry and Plentey came into the yard; he welcomed them.

"What's the matter with the sheep?" Adam Fry asked. Richard explained. How strange that Adam had never visited on this day before.

"Mr Fry's been giving me the London news," John Plentey said.

"I've just been telling Plentey about the Earl of Warwick's meeting with his old enemy, Queen Marguerite. It's the talk of London," said Adam.

"I don't see how Warwick could trust Marguerite or King Louis," John said.

Adam had been thinking about that. "King Louis knows Warwick of old. Each thinks he has the measure of the other. But Louis most likely has Warwick where he wants him. Where else could Warwick get help now?"

Both John and Simon looked amazed by this. Simon said, "You think King Louis can persuade Queen Marguerite to join forces with the man who has done most to vilify her?"

"The queen can do nothing at all without King Louis' backing," Richard reminded them.

"Queen Marguerite will find only suspicion and hostility in most parts of England," John said.

"Even so, John, there are many humble Lancastrian people who love King Harry still - perhaps half of all Englishmen. Edward cannot punish them all," Simon replied. "And I'll give the devil his due; he's never been a vindictive king."

"I believe Trencher's right," Adam said. "I think in their hearts about half our people love King Harry and the other half King Edward. At the same time, most of them can see the dilemma: the old king who showed himself so unfit to rule on the one hand, and on the other, the young upstart with a talent for leadership, who arguably has a rather better claim to the throne. A man in two minds symbolises the country torn in half. It's no wonder so many hesitate to commit themselves."

"It was rash of my Lord of Warwick to change sides," said Richard.

John replied, "It's an Englishman's privilege and sometimes his duty to change his mind. But you think Warwick's heading for disaster, Fry?"

"On balance, yes. But we mustn't underestimate him. He's surprised us all before." He paused, then said, "King Harry could be back on the throne in a few months' time with his sixteen-year-old son at his side."

"A new protégé for Warwick!" John said and they all laughed.

Lydia came out of the house with a pitcher. "Hullo Cousin, hullo Mr Plentey. You'll be needing more ale, Father." Richard poured ale for his guests.

Adam turned to Lydia. "I'm sure you're missing your friends now they're in Normandy, Lydia. I heard in London, just before I left, that Anne Neville is to be betrothed to Prince Edouard! Have you heard from her?"

Lydia nearly dropped the cup she was passing to John Plentey and turned to Adam.

"Oh no, Cousin, It can't be so! Anne is only fourteen and needs another year or so before such cares."

"Yes, she's very young, but her father wants to make a pact with Queen Marguerite and this is likely to be the only way they can trust each other."

"Poor Anne. She dreamed of a rich and handsome husband but not a royal one. And a wedding in the little church at Middleham, not in a French castle."

Lydia made sure each man's cup was replenished and went quietly back into the house. She felt a great cloud of sorrow. Anne was, after all, little more than a ewe-lamb herself. How could she bear to be made a sacrifice by her own father?

She recalled a day at Middleham when all three girls had been musing on the future. Anne had suddenly announced, "I shall be a rich widow!"

Isabel asked her where she got that idea.

"When Mother had a visit from that tall lady in the blue velvet gown, I listened at the door. She is having a huge house built full of all the latest conveniences. She told Mother that each of her elderly husbands had left her a vast fortune and she had the chance to create something beautiful! She could decide everything for herself without leaning on a man."

But now Anne could decide nothing for herself. Lydia went to bed with a heavy heart.

In the morning the cloud lifted and Lydia reflected that an idyllic childhood, such as Anne had had, made a sure foundation for facing life's storms.

Chapter 17
WARWICK LANDS AT DARTMOUTH

Rupert worked steadily on the pulpit through the summer. He was always up early to make the most of the daylight hours hoping to get the work finished before the winter.

September came and Tom was anxious to get the north aisle paved. The rest of the floor had been finished the previous year. He hurried into the church one morning looking for the men. "Cuthbert! There's a load of flagstones arrived from the quarry. Go and unload them, lad. You too, Jack. There's only one man with the cart and he's seeing to the horses. Joshua'll show you where to stack the stones."

Tom had other things on his mind too. He went over to Rupert's workbench.

"Rupert, are ye any good with figures? I've got all these prices to add up for the churchwardens and my work is interrupted every five minutes."

"I don't know about adding up, Tom. It's multiplication I'm good at. Hours of work times hourly rate."

"Then you can estimate the likely cost of your work on the pulpit; they'll want that too."

"It'll take another five weeks at least. I had expected to return to Windsor before winter. King Edward was making plans for a special chapel and I promised to work on it. But that'll be held up now that the Earl of Warwick is expected to land soon."

"Have you heard any more news?"

"One of Mr Fry's men arrived from London last night. King Edward is still in the North Country putting down rebellions; there is panic in the City of London and Warwick's fleet has been sighted in the Channel."

"The king is in danger then," Tom said. "I'd say he won't be building a chapel at Windsor for two or three years yet. It's my opinion King Edward should have arranged a quiet death for King Harry in the Tower before now. Without King Henry the Sixth, Warwick's rebellion would have no support. Marguerite and her boy cannot attract much of a following."

"I didn't know you followed politics, Tom."

"I keep me ears open."

"I'm not sure I agree with you. King Harry is mostly forgotten. News of his death would cause more interest; he'd be seen as a martyr." Their conversation was stopped abruptly by a loud scream. Tom started towards the door.

Cuthbert hurried in. "Jack's injured, Tom. Dropped a stone on 'is foot. I reckon 'e'll be 'oppin' on one leg fer a week or two."

A few days later Sir Gilbert de Villepion returned to Northleach. He arrived at Woolman's house one evening with a younger man he introduced as William Skinner. Woolman welcomed them.

"My Lord of Warwick needs me at his side," Sir Gilbert said. "In future Skinner will bring you news and orders."

"Has my lord landed in England?"

"My Lord of Warwick, the Earl of Oxford and Jasper Tudor have landed at Dartmouth and declared they come for King Harry. They sailed with a fleet of sixty ships. Some put in at Plymouth. The Earl of Warwick has at least twenty thousand men and marches to Coventry."

"So they avoided the gales."

Skinner said, "'Twas a gale ten days ago that blew away the king's blockading ships, sir. Just gave our fellows a chance to nip across when it died down."

"May I ask when Queen Marguerite is expected?"

"My lord has been urging her to sail before the end of September, but I fear the Channel is now filled with King Edward's ships," Sir Gilbert replied.

Skinner added, "And Jasper Tudor needs time to muster his Welshmen."

Woolman asked the question that was so important to Lydia. "And Clarence and his wife? Have they sailed to England?"

"Clarence was in one of the ships that docked at Plymouth. He should soon catch up with the army. I can't tell you whether his wife came with him. Now Skinner, give Mr Woolman his instructions."

"Yes, sir. We have one of our men engaged as a servant at the inn at Bibury, sir. If you need a messenger to ride to Coventry or London, you must get word to him. Ask for Jonathan."

"I'm glad of that. I should not like Joshua to take the risk again."

"You are still useful to my lord," Sir Gilbert said. Woolman didn't think anyone had doubted that. "Northleach is well placed on the road from Chepstow to London as well as the Fosse from Leicester to Exeter. And your pigeons help. Though only in one direction."

So he recognised Northleach's importance now, did he? But Woolman said only, "There are travellers of all sorts from London at this time of the year. News from there usually reaches me in a day or two."

"Would you keep a record for me of what you hear, sir? Your part is important you know," said Skinner.

Perhaps William would be a more congenial colleague. Woolman said, "It's a very small part, William, but I'll do my best."

After their departure Woolman told Lydia what they had said. She had implored him to confide in her, persuading him that combining their different experience they could together be more effective.

When Trencher came round later they discussed the situation with him. All were uneasy about the future of the country. What hope was there that Warwick would be able to agree with the Earl of Oxford and the Duke of Somerset, the two lords the queen trusted? The boy, Prince Edouard, was only sixteen; they would all try to influence him. There were the Welsh to consider too. Jasper Tudor had a mind of his own and thousands of loyal followers in Wales. He had more reason than most to hate King Edward.

Lydia's mind went back to the times at Middleham when the Earl of Warwick would come in after a long day out and sit a little while with his wife and children. He always made Lydia feel included. Sometimes he had a tale to tell of the day's excursion; often he joined in one of the word games devised by Isabel; at other times the girls' questions might start him on accounts of days gone by or explanations of the complicated relationships between the Nevilles, other lords, and the Royal Family. So Lydia knew the story of Jasper of Pembroke.

After the battle of Mortimer's Cross, ten years earlier, the victorious Edward had had Jasper's father, Owen Tudor, beheaded in Hereford market place. Jasper had been made Earl of Pembroke by King Henry but the title had been revoked by King Edward and given to William Herbert.

Jasper had French royal blood as well as Welsh. His mother was the late Queen Katherine, the widow of Henry the Fifth. His young nephew, Henry Tudor, of whom he was immensely proud, had even more royal blood; his mother, Lady Margaret Beaufort, was descended from John Beaufort, the eldest of the illegitimate children of John of Gaunt, who had eventually married his mistress, Katherine Swynford. The children had been legitimised but barred from the succession, an arrangement Jasper thought very grudging.

Woolman could not shake off his anxiety. That was something he was determined to keep from Lydia. Everything had been going well until Warwick had fallen out with the young king. If he couldn't fit in with Edward, what were his chances of working with the unpredictable French queen and her various argumentative supporters?

Chapter 18
KING EDWARD'S FLIGHT

One morning after the reading lesson, Lyda and Ellen discussed recent events.

"One of Mr Fry's men brought news from London last night. The Earl of Warwick has reached Coventry with an army of thirty thousand men," Lydia told Ellen.

"So the battle could come soon?"

"Apparently King Edward hasn't enough men until my Lord of Montagu arrives with his army. Montagu is Warwick's brother. He has been loyal to the king but now there are rumours he can't be relied on."

"Hast thou heard anything from Isabel?"

"No. When the army marched up the Fosse last week, George of Clarence must have been with them. I was wondering if he took Isabel as far as Warwick Castle. But then a letter arrived from Anne. One of Warwick's men must have brought it. She says Isabel is still with them in Normandy."

"The countess must be glad to have them both with her."

"Yes. Of course, Queen Marguerite insists Anne and her mother stay in Normandy. Anne says she has the title 'Princess of Wales'. Her comments on the queen are quite amusing. Prince Edouard is his mother's pride and joy. And he has stood godfather to Queen Charlotte's baby boy."

"I expect she must take care only to write of family matters."

"Yes. We shall have Cousin Fry here next week with more news. He's in Flanders, selling wool at the Michaelmas Fairs."

"And Hugh? Is he still in Calais?"

"I suppose so. I've heard nothing."

"I believe thou'rt missing him, Lydia."

"Yes, I'm surprised to find I am." Lydia had overheard two young girls in the market place discussing the charms of Hugh Plentey and other young men a few days earlier and had realised quite suddenly how much he mattered to her.

"I miss him more each day. Dost think he might be missing me? There must be plenty of girls in Calais."

"When I last saw the two of you together, I thought how animated you looked. He went away at the wrong moment."

"We had some good times but nothing was put into words. At first I thought that Robert was the more interested but I soon found I liked Hugh better."

Lydia was enjoying her visits to Mrs Plentey. She found her so different from herself and yet so easy to talk to. One lacked a mother, the other a daughter, but in no way did either try to replace the person missing. It was rather that their friendship filled a gap where an intimacy between the generations could benefit and delight both. Now and then Lydia saw Robert about the town; she was often told how well Hugh was doing in the business in Calais.

Lydia went round to the Plenteys' house one morning to find Mrs Plentey at the foot of the big apple tree in the garden with various baskets. She at once explained what each one contained. "These apples are windfalls; have you already too many from your own tree?" and without waiting for an answer continued to chatter, interrupting herself to direct operations upwards into the branches of the tree, where Andrew, the stable hand, was picking the fruit. He had filled a basket which he was about to lower. There was an ingenious system involving three baskets, a long loop of rope and several meat hooks.

"You can help me take the weight, Lydia," Mrs Plentey said, "then we needn't call Daisy this time." Daisy was the kitchen maid. Lydia helped pay out the rope steadily. The full basket came down and an empty one went up. The third basket was already full and its weight saved the whole exercise from getting out of hand. When the newly-filled basket had reached the ground safely, Mrs Plentey paused to wipe her hands on her apron. "Stop and sit with me, Lydia," she said. "You must try my gooseberry wine." Over the gooseberry wine, Mrs Plentey told Lydia how Robert and Hugh had invented the basket system two years ago when they last had a bumper crop.

Lydia found herself telling her friend that she was trying to help her father over the matter of the breeding records of the sheep. "Our old shepherd died last week, I expect you heard, Mrs Plentey. He was the only man who knew each ewe personally, the tups too. One of the other shepherds knows most of them and so does Joshua but nothing gets written down. I am trying to persuade Father that we should have written records if we are to improve the flock."

"You sound like Robert," Mrs Plentey said. "He has taken over the records of our flock for his father. We are so fortunate to have two sons in the business. Hugh does most of the travelling and helps my sister's son in Calais, while Robert likes to make sure everything is written down properly. Perhaps he could give you some help."

"I couldn't ask him. He must have more than enough to do already."

"I might happen to remark to him then, that it is a great interest of yours and how difficult it is without the knowledge of your old shepherd."

Indeed, it might be helpful to ask Robert about breeding records. But tupping time was almost upon them. They would have to leave it to Joshua to follow his own method of remembering which tup had covered each ewe.

A few days later, one of Adam Fry's men came to see Richard Woolman.

"Mr Fry wanted to be sure you had heard the latest news," he said.

"Has Warwick's army reached London?"

"He's well on the way. My news is that King Edward has been forced to flee to the Low Countries."

"God's nails!" Woolman exclaimed. "However did this come about?"

"Lord Montagu left the king and returned to his brother of Warwick. It is thought that about four hundred men got away with the king, including Richard of Gloucester. They hope to get help from the Duke of Burgundy or one of the other lords."

Woolman was stunned. It was only two weeks since Warwick had arrived in England.

Towards the end of October, Mrs Plentey went early to the bakery. "Two large loaves, please," she said to Ellen. "I have Hugh at home; thou wouldst think he'd been starved in Calais."

"I'm so glad for you, Mrs Plentey. Hugh must be good company."

"He is, and I need it with the news from London being so dreadful. One king flown abroad and the other still a prisoner in the Tower. And poor Queen Elizabeth, seeking sanctuary at Westminster, she's near her time, thou know'st."

Ellen put the bread into Mrs Plentey's basket. "Your bread. Three ha'pence please."

"Thank thee, Ellen." Mrs Plentey gave her the coins. "I'm sure the queen will have a son this time, after three daughters."

"I should think it's likely, Mrs Plentey. Is Hugh with you for long?"

"He doesn't tell me much. I expect he'll soon be needed back in Calais. He's doing very well in the counting house there."

"I hear King Henry was brought out of the Tower of London yesterday. He'll be looking forward to seeing his son."

"Who told thee? I find it hard to believe."

"Mr Fry came last night with news bulletins. I've got one here somewhere. Lydia read it to me. Shall I try to read it to you?" Ellen had some papers under the counter and soon found what she was looking for. She read it out carefully.

"King Henry is brought from the Tower and will be installed in the Palace of Westminster."

"Thou'rt reading well, Ellen."

"I have a good teacher. Reading is coming easily now. Writing is much more difficult. Shall I go on?"

"Is there more?"

Ellen began confidently but was soon stumbling over the long words. She kept steadily on.

"New coins will be struck, bearing King Henry's likeness. The Earl of Warwick's new title is 'Lieutenant to our Sovereign Lord, King Henry the Sixth.' He has appointed himself Great Chamberlain of England and Captain of Calais."

Mrs Plentey looked scornful. "My Lord of Warwick has a high opinion of himself. I'd think better of him if he'd stayed true to King Edward."

Chapter 19
A SON AND HEIR

The Vicar, alone in the church one morning, looked round more attentively than usual. All was quiet; very soon work would stop for the winter. Much of it seemed to be finished. He must ask Tom how far the woodcarvers had got with the screen. There seemed at last a ray of hope that all might be ready for Easter next year.

He returned home for his period of study and after reading part of the book of Acts found himself musing, as so often, on the contrast between St Peter and St Paul.

The two men could hardly be more different: Peter from the humble folk on the shore of the Lake of Galilee, Paul from a prosperous family in Tarsus; Peter, the skilled fisherman and, later, pastor; Paul, trained in his family's tent-making business, who had been sent to study in Jerusalem. Geoffrey could think of no Northleach man in either trade. Children were always fishing for what they could find in the River Leach, nothing of any size. But many people, on a festive occasion, had tasted Bibury trout from the River Coln.

As for tents, somebody must make the awnings that every stallholder used to protect his wares from rain and sun, and the covers for wagon loads. Besides, many merrymakers at the Fair, when the inns were full, slept in little tents, pitched on the Church Field; indeed they could hire them from Robin, the wheelwright.

He had been told that the tents came from a man in Stow and he had a memory too of a tentmaker in Gloucester, down near the docks, next to the sailmaker's shop.

During the few days before the frosts were expected, when work would come to a halt, Tom tried to make the church tidy for the winter months. Rupert prepared to return to Windsor, promising he would be back in the spring. He would walk down the path by the River Leach and hope to find a boatman at Lechlade willing to take him down the Thames.

There were several days of heavy rain. Even though the temperature hadn't dropped much, it felt cold enough.

Cuthbert was chopping wood one afternoon.

"I was thinking of starting a nice little business in kindling wood," he said to Jack. "But Tom says it's to be taken to the poor folk at the almshouses. If any is sold, the flaming money is to go the poor."

"I'm one o' the poor, I got no wages fer a month when me foot was bad."

Jack's foot was still bandaged, though he seemed to move freely enough.

With a flourish of his axe, Cuthbert said, "I could chop it off fer ye, if yer like. Be less farting trouble then."

Jack dodged the axe and picked up his own. "Stick to yer own work. Choppin's about all I can do at the moment."

Cuthbert straightened up and looked at Jack. "I've heard executioners are well-paid, I think I'll apply fer work at the goddam Tower o' London. Couldn't be worse than the ruddy work here."

"What? Cut off heads? They'd make yer clean up afterwards. All that blood!"

"Nah, they've other fellers to clean up. That's work you could do."

The church door burst open; Plentey and Woolman came in, having shaken the rain from their cloaks in the porch. They saw Jack waving his axe towards Cuthbert.

"We'll need to look out for these wild fellows, Richard! On with your work, boys! You don't know your own luck with indoor toil on a day like this." The two merchants had been caught by a sudden squall as they were about to pass the church.

"All my shepherds went out this morning," said Richard. "I hope they'll have found some cover."

"Each man'll have a fell on his back and be as dry as a sheep," John reminded him. "Let's have a good look round while we're out of the rain. I've heard Rupert has been carving the new pulpit."

They crossed the nave to look at the pulpit. "This is good work, John. Tom's been fortunate to find such a mason."

"I hear he's one of King Edward's best."

They became absorbed in studying the details of the carving. Jack and Cuthbert, quiet now, filled sacks with firewood. None of them noticed Joshua hurry in at the door at the foot of the tower and make for the stairs that led to the bell-ringers' loft.

Richard realised the drumming of the rain on the windows had eased. "How quiet it is now," he said. "Do you remember all the noise when the work began, when we were young boys? Those great hammers swinging when the pillars were demolished. And the crash of rubble thrown into carts!"

"And the clouds of dust! And here we are, able to see the work being finished."

"Your father and mine talked about it all their lives."

They heard the click of the latch as Simon Trencher came in through the porch door. At the same time Tom emerged from the Vicar's little room off the chancel. John took the opportunity of a quiet word with Tom while Richard walked towards Simon.

"What some weather!" said Simon. "I've come to collect the latest bills from Tom."

"I'd been hoping to see thee. I wanted to tell thee my cousin Fry was here yesterday and told me Jasper Tudor is in London, visiting King Henry."

Tom came up to them with the papers Simon wanted, John following him. They had overheard.

Richard told them, "Jasper took his young nephew, Henry Tudor, to see the king, and also to visit his mother, Lady Margaret Beaufort."

"I believe the boy's been a long time in Wales," said Simon, "and Jasper in France. Quite a family reunion."

John said, "Can you see Queen Marguerite and her boy fitting into English life now?"

"No, she won't be popular," said Simon. "But Warwick has a huge army and Jasper will raise the Welshmen. How can King Edward ever prosper again? He's not even on this side of the Channel."

"I'm anxious for our poor country, Simon," said John, "it's hard to watch England being torn in half."

Suddenly the bass bell rang. The sound echoed round the church and startled them all.

"Have we a new bell-ringer?" Richard asked.

"Where are those lads - are they fooling around again? I told them not to touch the bells."

John knew what the sound meant. "A son and heir for King Edward!"

Simon said, "Tom, I came in to tell you that Mr Plentey had asked if the bell might be rung when news of the birth came from London - if it was a boy. I asked Joshua to be ready."

Joshua appeared and hurried towards them, slightly out of breath. "It's all right, Tom, a fellow I know has just arrived from London. He's reliable, Mr Trencher. He said Queen Elizabeth was delivered of a fine boy yesterday."

"'Tis a good omen, Mr Plentey. We may not have so long to wait after all," said Tom.

John Plentey appeared to be overjoyed. "King Edward has an English Queen and now an English Prince. That's what we need. I hope my Lord of Warwick takes that to heart!"

Richard and Simon looked at each other. "Poor Warwick, his lady never bore him a son," said Richard. Both were thinking the same was true of them.

Chapter 20
ANNE'S MARRIAGE

In December, a package was brought to Lydia by a messenger from Exeter. News at last. She read the contents quickly, then put on her cloak and hurried round to the bakery. Ellen welcomed her in and made a hot drink for them both, an infusion of mint leaves, dried last summer. They sat at the kitchen table; Lydia spread the papers out.

"I've had two letters," she said. "This one's from Isabel. She's only recently arrived from Normandy." She began to read it aloud.

> "Anne and Prince Edouard were married on the 13th of December in the King's Chapel at Amboise. Anne looked really beautiful. She has grown taller since you saw her. The Grand Vicar of Bayeux officiated. He was the man King Louis had sent to visit the Eastern Orthodox Patriarch of Jerusalem who provided the dispensation for the marriage of the two cousins. Father could not be with us. He sent George to stand in his place and give Anne away. We had to leave the next day as the favourable wind was not likely to last. It was as well that George insisted that I come. I could never have decided myself to leave Mother and Anne at Amboise. That was the hardest thing of all."

Lydia paused and said, "It's hard for the countess too. She always kept close to my lord on his travels.

They will be lost without each other." She went on reading.

"I look forward to seeing Father when I get to London. Uncle Archbishop is in charge of King Henry at Westminster Palace. George is unsettled by letters from his sister in Burgundy. She and the duke are living at Damme, not far from The Hague where King Edward and Richard of Gloucester are lodged with the Governor of Holland. We are resting today in Exeter and start for London tomorrow.

Isabel always feels at home in Exeter," Lydia explained to Ellen. "George Neville, Warwick's brother, was Bishop of Exeter before he was made Archbishop of York. The family was often welcomed at the Bishop's Palace when the girls were young."

Lydia turned the page. "She says at the end of the letter,

Father wants George to take me to Burford for a while. That's not far from you, is it?"

Lydia was thoughtful for a minute. "I expect he wants her out of London but not too far from Coventry."

"So at last thou mightst see her."

"I do hope so. That letter was written on the fifteenth. This note from Anne was enclosed. Do thou read it to me, Ellen. Her handwriting is easier to read than Isabel's." She handed the single sheet to Ellen.

"Dear Lyddie, Two pigeons arrived yesterday. How clever of thee to sew thy note into the lid of the basket. Prince Edouard is handsome and he's kind to me but he doesn't understand my jokes. I enjoy our rides together. He let me try his horse yesterday. I have never been up so high before. We have to have the bodyguard, Gaston, with us, but he's a nice man and not fussy. I've been told to forget what the Queen did to Grandfather but the harder I try to forget, the more I remember."

Ellen paused. "What was that?" she asked Lydia.

"The queen's army won the Battle of Wakefield and she had two men's heads stuck on the spikes above the Micklegate in York. The heads of Warwick's and Edward of York's fathers. That used to make a bond between Warwick and Edward."

"No wonder the king feels his old friend has betrayed him." Ellen resumed her reading.

"Mother is missing Father. It was so much better when we were all together. I can't say what I really think to my mamma any more - I have to try to boost her courage. I can share jokes with my maid, Connie. Do you remember her at Middleham? But she's terrified of the queen so really I'm propping her up too. The man who is looking after the pigeons let me feed them yesterday. I held one in my hands and thought what a miracle it is that if I tossed it into the sky, it would fly straight to your house in Northleach. The picture is for your father. I hope he likes it. Lots of hugs and kisses from Anne."

Ellen put down the letter and asked Lydia to show her the picture.

"Father will like this. It's a beautiful drawing of his favourite pigeon."

1471

Chapter 21
THE KING HAS LANDED

On a spring afternoon, Lydia coaxed the old dog to accompany her up on the hills. There was no danger now that he would be tempted to show her how well he could round up sheep; he was far too stiff. She took him up the valley above the spot where centuries earlier the springs had been diverted to form the millstream, while the old riverbed in the valley bottom had become dry except at times of exceptional rainfall. The busily grazing sheep were spread across the bright new grass.

Hugh Plentey was out walking too; he saw Lydia higher up and easily overtook her. She did not hear him coming and was suddenly alerted by the vigorous tail-wagging of her companion.

As she turned, Hugh said, "Lydia! I hoped I might find you up here."

"Hugh! I thought you were in Calais. What a surprise."

Spontaneously they took each other's hands and stood looking intently at each other. Both were surprised by the surge of emotion. Hugh recovered first.

"You're looking fit and well; I'd hoped you might be missing me."

Lydia removed her hands from his. "Why's that? You've not been away long, have you?"

"No, just since Christmas, about eleven weeks." It seemed long enough to Hugh.

"Is there any news? I've heard nothing from Isabel. I suppose Anne and her mother must be making ready to sail to England with Queen Marguerite."

"So you haven't heard that King Edward has landed on the Yorkshire coast?"

"Really? I never thought he'd come so soon."

"It was three days ago," Hugh said, "London is a-buzz with the news. But the king has only a small army."

"And my Lord of Warwick?"

"He's in Coventry with a huge army, ready to do battle soon."

"I wonder if Isabel is there. She wrote last in January, from London."

"Clarence has been raising men in the West Country. She may be in Exeter. The Earl of Oxford has landed in Devon; Jasper Tudor is mustering his Welsh army. King Edward's spies must know all that."

Lydia realised the dog had sat down and was wearing his 'time to go home' expression. They turned back towards the town, the dog going ahead.

"And you, Hugh? Will you be here for a while?"

"No. I wanted to tell you: I will be joining Warwick's army."

"Does he really need you, too?"

"I can't stand aside, Lyddie." She had never heard him use the familiar form of her name before. "Now I have to decide how to break it to Mother and Father. You see, Robert has joined King Edward's army. I had a letter from him while I was in Calais. He said he was ready to join the king as soon as he heard he had landed."

"Oh Hugh!"

"I'd like to talk to your father before I see mine. Would he mind, do you think? I know he supports Warwick and mine does not."

"He'd be glad to see you. Come back with me now." They had nearly reached the road and she broke into a run; the dog tried to copy her but trailed behind them both. She took Hugh straight to the yard and into the house at the back. Richard Woolman was startled to see them but welcomed Hugh gladly.

"Good day to you, sir," Hugh said. "I found Lydia out walking and asked to have a few words with you."

"I'll leave you to it, I have errands to run," said Lydia.

"I must give you the latest news, sir. King Edward has landed on the Yorkshire coast."

Richard was surprised; he had heard nothing of this from Will Skinner.

"You've come from London?"

"Yes. The news had just come when I arrived there. Everyone is discussing it. It's uncertain whether the king can raise more than a few men."

"I believe my Lord of Warwick has a large following."

"Sir, may I ask you... er, do you think, sir..."

"What's on your mind, Hugh?"

"I know you support Warwick, sir. Yet you keep friends with my father. I admire Warwick so much. I wondered..."

"I owe him a great deal, Hugh. I would do anything to help my lord."

"I thought you would understand. I feel I must join Warwick's army."

"Are you sure you're ready for this? Northleach men have no obligation."

"I've thought it over for some time, sir. I don't quite know how to tell my father. Robert has left to join King Edward's army. Mother must be worried enough already."

Woolman looked concerned. "They will find it hard, but they will understand that each man must choose his own path."

"I hope you're right, sir. I have to report at Coventry in three days' time."

"Call here before you leave, Hugh. I may have news for you to take with you. And you could take a pigeon to bring a message here."

The following week, Will Skinner came to see Woolman. He told him that the Duke of Somerset had left for the south coast to be ready to meet Queen Marguerite on her arrival. He had sent most of his men to join the Earl of Warwick at Coventry but kept a small force with him. There were reports from Normandy that the queen was fully prepared and awaited only a favourable wind. She had three thousand men provided by King Louis, while Jasper Tudor was on his way to muster thousands of Welshmen. Jasper had recently been over to Normandy, Will said, and tried to persuade Queen Marguerite to make for Milford Haven or another of the Welsh ports. But she hated sea voyages and was determined to make the shortest possible crossing from Harfleur. The wind would probably determine her place of arrival. Somerset had men at Plymouth, Dartmouth, Weymouth, Southampton and Portsmouth and messengers ready to travel between the ports on horseback. The queen would bring her young son with her, on whom she pinned all her hopes, and of course his very young wife, Anne Neville. Keeping Anne close to her ensured Warwick's continued loyalty. Jasper had urged her to come soon; every day lost meant King Edward was better prepared.

Will had to ride back to the south coast next day. He went round to the Red Lion to get a good night's sleep, promising to call early in the morning for a pigeon.

Chapter 22
BURFORD

Lydia received a letter from Isabel saying that she and George of Clarence were taking a few days at the house in Burford and could Lydia possibly come over to see her.

Richard Woolman realised how much this meant to his daughter and arranged that Joshua should escort her and take some business letters for him to Burford. Joshua could easily be spared; lambing was just beginning but the shepherds would not be under pressure for another week. One of Adam Fry's men was in Northleach and was given a letter confirming the arrangements, to take to Isabel on his way back to London.

Next day was fine and warm for the last week in March and the two set out early. The air was full of birdsong which mingled with occasional sheep calls. The blackthorn was out; tiny white stars dotting the hedges. The horses made their way up the hill out of the Leach valley and took the road for Sherborne, a long straggling village with a shallow brook which was soon to flow into the River Windrush. Lydia had been here before to see the sheep washing. The next village took its name from the river. They passed the church, dipped downhill to the river then climbed a little on the same bank to Little Barrington where they found the track with views across the valley. This brought them into Burford near the Warwick family home.

Isabel had posted a man at the gate to take the horses and a maid to bring Lydia up the drive.

Joshua went off on foot to visit Woolman's business acquaintance and his lawyer. At last the two girls were together again.

"Oh Lyddie," said Isabel, embracing her, "welcome. It's so good to see thee. I have some ale and cold meat ready for us in this room and when thou art rested I plan to take thee through the garden and down to see the river."

"I wondered if I would ever see thee again!" said Lydia.

Isabel took her into a large reception room. She felt suddenly a little shy. Isabel was a duchess now - the room seemed grand and was very beautifully furnished. Isabel saw Lydia's discomfiture at once and began to chatter to her just as she would have done in the schoolroom at Middleham. She asked after Lydia's father and was just beginning to express her anxiety over her own father's sending Lydia such a demanding message, when a servant came in to make up the fire and another to see if they had all the refreshments required.

Isabel began telling her amusing anecdotes about the time after Lydia left. They were soon laughing.

When, for a moment, the servants were all out of the room, Isabel said, "It's good of thee to come, Lyddie. It's not yet two years since we left Middleham but so much has happened."

"Oh Bel! I have so longed to see thee. Hast thou been keeping well, and thy husband?"

"I am fit but a little anxious about Mother and Anne. Poor George is in turmoil. We'll speak of that later." She went on to talk of their strange life in Normandy, dependent on the French king and on strained terms with the queen who was King Harry's wife. "Mother was so patient," said Isabel. "She said we must remember that Queen Marguerite has been separated from King Harry for several years while he's been a prisoner in the Tower of London. But I think all the queen's devotion was for her rather spoilt son, the young prince. Mother, of course, was sorry for him too. He had hardly known his father and here was his mother building up fantasies about his becoming King of England. It's a foreign land to him, though he has learned something of it from his tutors and has applied himself to his studies. And poor Mother, missing Father and facing so much uncertainty."

She asked Lydia about her friends in Northleach and whether there were any likely young men there. Lydia told her about Ellen and admitted she was attracted to Hugh Plentey and told her friend about the two brothers joining opposing armies.

They finished their meal and Isabel said, "There are too many people in this house with sharp ears. Dost thou feel ready for a walk?" She rang for the maid who brought back Lydia's cloak and her own and they started down a path that led to the bank of the River Windrush.

When they were well clear of the house, Isabel told Lydia about her husband's troubles.

"Poor George is very anxious," she said. "He hasn't said much but I'm sure he's turning over in his mind whether he should make peace with his brother. You see, all the noblemen who support King Harry are disdainful and suspicious of George and it hurts."

"I suppose his sisters are still persuading him to stand by his brother?"

"Yes. I was hoping a rest here in Burford would calm him. But he can't find any rest. I love it here. He's out hunting today with a few loyal men; it may calm his mind and give him a chance to think. He has to decide soon because Father is expecting him in Coventry. He's inside Coventry city walls; he can keep more men safe there than at Warwick Castle."

They came out from the trees. There were daffodils growing on the edge of the woodland, a meadow stretched ahead sloping gently to the swiftly-flowing river. Isabel was pleased at her friend's gasp of delight.

"Our River Leach is such a little brook compared with this," Lydia said. She asked whether Isabel had heard from her mother or Anne.

"Not for a while," Isabel said. "Mother's messages go to Father. Sometimes he remembers to send them on to me. Poor Father, the birth of Queen Elizabeth's son was a great blow. His plan was for King Edward to be killed in battle. Now he has a male heir there's not much point. George, of course, is jealous of Queen Marguerite's son, Prince Edouard, now that Father plans power for him in the future and not for George."

"No... I can see there's nothing for George now."

"While King Edward was in Holland, he sent a woman to visit me to ask for my help in persuading George to return to him. At about the same time, he, the king, sent a letter to Queen Marguerite, so Father told me recently, asking her to put the peace of the realm of England first and make a marriage alliance between Prince Edouard and his eldest daughter Elizabeth, who is seven years old."

"I wonder if that could have worked," Lydia said.

"It sounds unlikely doesn't it? Anyway, the queen is under the influence of King Louis. He is keeping her from poverty; Edward was not even in England. He could promise her nothing."

"Elizabeth is the pretty child who sometimes played in the nursery at Middleham!"

"Yes, I was thinking of those happy days too. King Louis was very suspicious of the offer from King Edward knowing that Edward might at any time have support from Burgundy. Louis would only make an alliance with England if he received support against Burgundy."

"And King Edward needs an alliance with Burgundy to keep in with London's merchants; he depends on many of them for loans of money."

"That's right. And it suits King Louis well to have

two factions in England tearing each other apart."

"Oh Bel! Will it ever end?"

They fell silent. Lydia looked back at the way they had come. It was a beautiful view of the swiftly-flowing river and the water meadows, the little town in the background with its church steeple. She thought she saw a man standing in the trees. Isabel looked up.

"I'm always watched," she said. "It's for my own safety, Lyddie. They don't come too close."

They began to walk again, up-river. Lydia said, "Dost thou think I should tell my father that George is likely to support his brother?"

"Oh no, Lyddie, thou couldst not do that. That's between thee and me." She looked quite distressed. "I have no-one else I can talk to."

"Bel! I didn't mean to upset thee!"

Isabel wasn't listening. "If I can't talk to thee, in whom shall I put my trust?" They looked at each other and smiled. The tension was broken. Lydia grasped Isabel's hands, saying, "Father Matthew at Middleham!"

They began to recite together, "In whom shall I put my trust? I will trust in the Lord..."

Isabel broke off. "So that's why he had us learn it by heart. He knew the words would be with us if trouble came."

Lydia went on, "Trust in the Lord with all your heart and lean not on your own understanding."

Isabel joined in, "In all your ways acknowledge Him and He will guide you on your path."

"Dear Father Matthew," Isabel said, "I suppose he is still at Middleham, visiting the sick, teaching the children..."

"And still giving comfort and hope to us. I won't let thee down, Bel."

They began the walk back to the house. It would soon be time for Lydia's departure.

"I don't suppose I'll see thee for a while," Isabel

said. "I'll try to write when I can. But Lyddie, I'm anxious about Mother and Anne. I may not be able to write to them. Can you send them a message to say I'm in good health?"

"That should be possible. We expect Queen Marguerite at any time now and they're certain to come with her. We'll be in constant touch, once they're in England."

Isabel suddenly seemed lost and vulnerable. "How's it going to end?" she said softly. "King Edward's sure to win the next battle, isn't he? I may be moving to the winning side. What'll happen to Anne on the other side? And to thee and thy father?"

"Be brave, darling. I shall be thinking of thee every day. It'll be all over soon." But Lydia didn't feel as brave as she sounded.

Isabel remembered there was something important that must be said.

"Lyddie, I must tell thee about the Code Book. Anne and I discussed it the day before her wedding. It was the last time we spent together. Supposing one of the books fell into the wrong hands. I must explain to thee how we altered it to make it safer." Her explanation of their ingenious idea for the code's safety took up the time till they reached the garden door of the house.

A servant told them that Joshua was ready at the gate with the horses. They said goodbye cheerfully, each trying to be brave for the sake of the other.

Chapter 23
THE SCREEN

Lydia was lost in her own thoughts as she and Joshua made their way back to Northleach. Joshua wasn't surprised. What a contrast there must be between her two lives, he thought to himself; one in Northleach, the other with the noble family in Yorkshire. He had heard Lydia speak of Isabel and Anne and knew how deeply attached she was to them. He had plenty to think about himself; he was looking forward to the new season of building work, with its promise of completion of the church in the coming months, but first there would be lambing, when he would take his turn to go out at night to check the ewes. And his own wife was expecting another child soon.

Lydia went straight to the kitchen where Margery warmed up the remains of the afternoon meal for her. She had assured her father it would be better not to wait for her to share it with him but she had not foreseen that she would be trying to avoid him for fear of the questions he would ask. She thought of Anne in Normandy; perhaps, after all, no child could share everything with a parent.

When she had eaten, she slipped out and began to walk across the market place. It was cold and she needed to be out of the wind while she thought over what Isabel had said. She made for the church. The door from the porch made its usual click though she tried to quieten it. She looked up, there was no-one there. She walked a few steps towards the nave and was startled by the colourful scene before her. In the late afternoon light she wondered if it was a dream but as she walked a little nearer she realised that the rood screen, that had been away so long being restored, had been set up in its place before the chancel arch. It was not quite complete, but most of the painting and gilding was finished. The screen filled almost the full width of the church. The steps in the wall that would connect with the loft had been scrubbed, but the loft was yet to come. Each panel bore a brightly painted portrait of one of the saints. She touched the robe of one, very cautiously; the paint looked wet but was dry.

Lydia was completely taken out of herself. Her anxiety about Isabel fell away. The church had seemed a dingy, colourless place for so long. She remembered Isabel saying, when they were about sixteen years old, that God was much more real up on the moors than in a dusty old church and she had been inclined to agree. But now, look what the craftsmen of Northleach had made to the glory of God. She walked slowly past each of the panels and then stood a long time, lost in thought.

The light was fading. She was startled by a shout and turned to see Simon Trencher coming towards her.

"Lydia, it's you!" he said. "It's my turn to lock up and we always call out, 'Anyone there?' for fear of locking people in for the night."

She laughed. She had been brought back to earth with a bump but she couldn't think of anyone she would rather see just then. She knew he would understand without her telling him a word.

"The screen looks new," she said to him as they walked back to the market place, "but I know they have been restoring the old one."

"Yes, Tom says he'll need all the time between now and Easter to finish it. While we're having this dry spell, it seemed important to carry the sections over from the barn. Most of it is here now and they can do the rest of the painting in the church, when the weather warms up a bit."

They said goodnight and Lydia went in to see her father, telling him excitedly about the screen and asking him if he had seen it. Richard Woolman had not told his daughter what Will Skinner had said a few days before: that there seemed to be a strong likelihood that George of Clarence would desert his father-in-law and return to his brother the king, taking all his men with him. He knew Lydia wanted to share all his information but the matter of George and Isabel was too delicate; he would wait till she herself was ready to speak of it.

They had no need to avoid this conversation for long; three days later it was the gossip of the market place. A trader had brought a message from London that George, Duke of Clarence, had changed sides.

Lydia wrote a letter for Anne and her mother and the next time Will Skinner called she asked him if he could get it to them as soon as they landed in England. He promised to keep it safe till then. She agonised over the pain they would feel when they knew that the terrible struggle for the throne of England was now dividing their own family.

To calm herself she would go into the garden, take some deep breaths and recall the words of St Paul that the Vicar had read to them last Sunday: 'Fill your mind with whatever is holy and just, true, pure and beautiful.' Like the walk with Isabel by the River Windrush or the manmade beauty of the painted screen in the fading light.

Chapter 24
WAITING

Richard Woolman sat at his counting house desk staring out of the window. He was thankful that most of the lambs had been born alive and were healthy and strong. Only a few ewes remained who were yet to give birth. He was relieved and satisfied that lambing had gone so well. All the shepherds had been paid and his funds should last till the payments from his customers in the Low Countries came through. Adam Fry was bound for the Easter Mart in Bruges where he would be collecting all the money due. Richard could rely on Adam to work out the various rates of exchange to get the best outcome.

At the same time, he was a little anxious because he still had much of last year's wool in store. It would need to be dispatched in time for the Whitsun Markets. Sheep shearing would begin soon after Whitsun; the store had to be cleaned ready for the new wool. Wool trains were leaving every few days but the last time he was ready with wool packed to go he had had difficulty finding enough horses. The wool fleet had been busy for a fortnight, cargoes bound for Calais leaving from many of the Thames wharves below London Bridge. The weather had been favourable since the spring gales died down.

Now everything would be interrupted by the Easter Holiday, but Adam's packers were due to come again as soon as it was over.

The whole town was in a bustle to be ready for Easter. It was always so, but this year there was an excitement in the air, with the nave ready at last for the Easter service. Richard felt a twinge of guilt when he thought how his own problems were making it so difficult for him to focus on Easter.

Always at the back of his mind was the thought of the part he was supposed to be playing in the Earl of Warwick's campaign. The previous day Will Skinner had taken most of his pigeons saying they were needed at the south coast ports so that news of Queen Marguerite's arrival could reach Northleach quickly. He was aware too of Lydia's longing to know that Anne Neville was safe in England. Lydia went quietly about her duties but Richard knew that she was trying not to show him her anxiety for Anne and also for Isabel in her change of loyalty from her father to her husband.

Richard's old friend Simon tried to offer sympathy and reassurance but for once Richard felt too weighed down to unburden himself. His deeper anxiety lay in his commitment to spy for the Earl of Warwick. It worried him more and more that it put Lydia in danger and threatened his whole way of life as a wool merchant. How had he got so involved?

He had met the earl and countess only once, at the time they had offered to take Lydia into their family as a companion for Isabel. Certainly he had a loyalty to them. But it was different now that such a deep rift had opened between Warwick and King Edward. Richard was uneasy that he was expected to favour a new reign by King Henry the Sixth and Queen Marguerite. He remembered only too well the turmoil caused by that woman in the past and the sudden changes in the health of King Henry which had often left him unfit to rule.

Now that Warwick's son-in-law, the unreliable George of Clarence, had changed sides, taking his thousands of men to join King Edward's army, Warwick and his friends were suddenly more vulnerable, while Isabel's duty was being sorely tested.

Will Skinner had discussed the change with him and told him that besides Warwick's grievous depletion of his forces he would have a great uneasiness and sense of isolation because he was not much liked by Somerset and Oxford, the English lords closest to the French queen.

It had all come to a head last week when King Edward reached the Midlands on his long march from York, with more support growing as he travelled. The Earl of Warwick was reported to be still in Coventry. King Edward, mindful of the terrible devastation of battle, was determined to make one last attempt at reconciliation. The earl had refused to come out from the city of Coventry so the king had marched to the nearby town of Warwick and made himself and his companions comfortable in the castle.

Will told Richard that the king had made two more approaches to the earl on successive days with no result. It was then that the Duke of Clarence had come to Edward, knelt before him and sworn his loyalty. The king had received his brother gladly and without further delay, and now at the head of a much larger army, had prepared to march to London.

He had gone straight to Westminster where Queen Elizabeth was living in sanctuary with her children and there he had seen his five-month-old son for the first time. The merchants of the City of London welcomed the king; they were genuinely pleased to see him and they were many of them his creditors, hoping they might have their loans repaid.

Will said that King Henry had been easily recaptured and returned to the Tower with instructions he was to be well treated. Clarence's wife, Isabel, had asked to see King Edward. The king had spoken gently to her, sensitive to her plight, but Queen Elizabeth would have nothing to do with her.

The Earl of Warwick waited a little longer in Coventry; he was not ready to march to London. The loss of Clarence and his men had made him even more cautious. Even so, he knew he must strike before King Edward built up a much larger army; it was too risky to wait for Queen Marguerite's landing. On the day before Will Skinner's visit to Northleach, Warwick ordered the march to the capital.

Richard's mind turned suddenly to John Plentey and his wife. He was guilty now of showing too little consideration for them with their two sons training in opposing armies. He was on his knees offering a prayer for Robert and Hugh when he heard his old dog greet Lydia as she came in by the yard gate.

Chapter 25
EASTER

Lydia had been up at the church helping with the preparations for Easter. The previous day she had visited Mrs Plentey and asked if she had heard anything of Robert or Hugh. She had not. She was doing her best to keep her spirits up for her husband's sake, but Lydia could see the strain in her face.

"Will you come with us tomorrow, Lydia, to the church?" Mrs Plentey had said. "Tom is getting everything clean for Easter and he suggested we women go in to see where we will put the Easter flowers and whether there is anything else to be done to be ready for the service."

It would be the first service in the nave for many years.

Lydia and Ellen met the other women early in the morning. Some of them had been in and out of the church for weeks but only Lydia had seen the screen, for it had been covered in sheets while the dust was swept up.

During Lent, Mrs Plentey had been there only for the Sunday services in the south aisle. Ellen was with her as she went into the nave.

"Oh Ellen, isn't it beautiful!" she said. "Tom, you have done such wonderful work."

"The dust is still in me eyes and nose, Mrs Plentey. Three of us have been up most of the night sweeping and scrubbing."

They all began to wander round, marvelling at what they saw.

Lydia said, "I've never seen a window over a chancel arch anywhere else, Tom; it's most unusual."

"Old Mr Plentey described to me a window he'd seen in Gloucester Abbey. This was his special wish."

"You have brought his vision to life, Tom," Mrs Plentey said.

And Lydia added, "I wish he could have seen it."

"There were such arguments about it, Lydia. Old Mr Plentey had trouble persuading your grandfather. For a long while old Mr Woolman wouldn't hear of having the nave altered. He said it looked well as it was, with the old tower and the new porch. I told him the old columns were Norman and no more kin to the tower and porch than our new work is."

"I love the new windows against the old tower, Tom." said Ellen.

"You must tell Mr Plentey so; he is all for rebuilding the tower! He's heard they're building a new one at Chipping Campden."

"Surely there'll be no more rebuilding just yet, Tom," said Mrs Plentey. Her husband had not told *her* he would favour a new tower.

"The finishing work we still have to do will see me to the end of my time. They'll need a younger man to oversee the work if they want a new tower. It'll take a couple of years to finish the north aisle. And now the churchwardens are discussing larger windows for the south aisle!"

Ellen was looking at the screen. "I can't believe it's not new, Tom."

"It is the old one, repaired and repainted. They're a fine team of carvers and painters who've been working on it for over two years. Now ladies, come through into the chancel and tell me if everything is there that we need for Easter Day."

The women had brought pots and vases and altar cloths and materials for polishing the church's silver vessels and candlesticks. Between them they decided who should bring flowers and budding branches and where they should be put. Ellen had to hurry back to the shop but Lydia stayed to help Mrs Plentey.

Everyone was excited about the fresh look of the old church but there was an underlying anxiety about the battle that was sure to come. News came that the Earl of Warwick's army was marching towards London.

Lydia was tormented by her anxiety for Hugh, about to fight against his own brother. Her heart ached too for Isabel, who in keeping loyal to her husband was forsaking her father, mother and sister.

The Vicar was distressed by the terrible split between Christians, even in his own small town. He knew that the people as a whole depended on a great battle to decide between the two factions and that they would abide by the decision and be thankful if that could be the end of the conflict. A terrible price would have to be paid and he prayed that some other way might be found to resolve the matter. For once he doubted the power of his prayers and his ability to give reassurance to those who asked him for help.

He re-read the Easter story in St John's Gospel as he did every year. He took it slowly and meditated on each verse. The monks had always been accustomed to conjure up each scene in the imagination.

When Jesus toiled up the hill carrying the great beam of the Cross, was he also weighed down by doubts and uncertainties? Geoffrey tried hard to imagine the pain. Had Jesus done all that the Father expected of him? Had he been faithful to the plan? Would these ordinary folk, his disciples, find the strength to carry on his work?

This train of thought once again brought Geoffrey to contemplate the characters of Peter and Paul, the saints of Northleach Church. Peter, known so well to the Lord Jesus. Impulsive Peter, sometimes missing the point of the message, fearful of what was about to happen; Peter who, when asked by strangers, denied all knowledge of Him because of his fear and bewilderment; who nevertheless had shown his devotion by leaving home and family and fishing business.

And Paul, not known personally to Jesus, but one of the group of Pharisees who had tried to trip him up and had become the persecutors of the disciples; Paul, known then as Saul, a man of standing in Jerusalem, surely the least likely to turn into a Follower of the Way; Paul, the educated Roman citizen from Tarsus, probably from a well-regarded family.

Paul, Peter and the other disciples seemed such unpromising material for the work that lay ahead. Geoffrey realised that he himself and all the faithful people he knew were equally unpromising material. Were the stories about the disciples there to give encouragement? On Easter Day he must tell his congregation, when he stood for the first time in the new pulpit, that every faithful person would be of value.

In the days leading up to Easter, all had to make their confession. A few of the older people kept the tradition of 'creeping to the Cross' on their knees on Good Friday. The women made an Easter Sepulchre as they had always done but lavished extra care on it. The rood loft was in place now. The young men in the band brought their pipes and drums and whistles to practise their tunes and hoisted old Phil, the nearly blind musician, up the steep steps with his lute.

Easter Day was warm with an early mist. The sun broke through just before the morning service. The bright, newly-growing grass could not quite hide the churchyard's carpet of celandines, and those who looked closely could see below them an underlay of violets.

Ellen had made herself a new gown from fine woollen cloth, dyed a light blue, woven from their own Cotswold wool and brought back from Flanders by the packhorses. Lydia took out a gown of chestnut brown velvet Isabel had given her. Isabel had tried it on, found it rather too large and realised that it didn't suit her. 'You try it, Lyddie,' she had said. It was just right for Lydia with her rosy cheeks and dark eyes. She had worn it only once before. She was pleased to see her father in his second best furred gown. He never wore his best, but kept it for some special occasion which had not yet materialised.

Everyone was there; the church was packed. All those who had been too ill or too old to come to church through much of the winter had been visited and helped to take their places. Tom came in with the masons, woodcarvers and labourers and all were congratulated after the service for their particular work.

Lydia was calmed by the old liturgy and soothed by the music. The little band of musicians made a more rounded and joyful sound now they were nearer the roof timbers and suddenly it seemed that everyone could sing angelically. The Vicar found a renewed confidence as, at the end of the Mass, he read the opening passage of St John's Gospel in Latin. He then summarised it in English though he knew that many people understood some of the Latin words.

"In the Beginning was the Word. The Word was in God's presence; and what God was, the Word was. He existed with God at the beginning and through Him all things were created; none was made without Him. In Him was Life and that Life was the Light of Mankind. The Light still shines in the darkness and the darkness has never overcome it."

For a few moments all was quiet and the birds could be heard outside. Then the Vicar gave his closing blessing and began to walk slowly to the door.

Simon Trencher opened it and the more distant sounds of sheep bells could be heard, soon to be drowned by a joyful chorus from the musicians and the pealing of the church bells. Each person in the congregation made a little bow to the Vicar or shook his hand and as they spilled out into the sunshine they greeted their neighbours. The children dashed about the churchyard and played leapfrog over the smaller gravestones until reprimanded by their elders.

Mr and Mrs Plentey were arm in arm. "What a lovely day, John! And a beautiful service in our new church!"

"Yes, it's a dream come true, after all these years."

"John, I'm praying for safety for our boys. May we all be together for Pentecost."

"Amen to that." John tried to feel brave but he was weighed down with sadness. So much trouble and pain would have been prevented if only the Earl of Warwick had worked with King Edward for the good of everyone. Just as the church his father had dreamed of and worked so hard for had become a reality, and as the king he supported seemed to have a real chance of victory, he could feel only anxiety and grief.

Richard Woolman, following days of worry and broken nights, had been calmed and comforted by the Easter service. He turned to his friend, Simon. He said with a chuckle, "I liked the Vicar's prayer, 'God save the king and queen and all those with earthly authority.' He has always named the king and queen before."

"He told me he prayed long and hard over what he should say. He has come to believe that only a battle can show us the rightful king now."

"Last Sunday, I said amen to 'God save King Edward the fourth and Queen Elizabeth.' What will it be next Sunday?"

"First I think one and then the other," Simon said.

- 119 -

Quietened and moved by the service, Richard found that he could take a more detached view now. He would prefer not to be a spy... and yet he found the unfolding story strangely fascinating. But it was hard to think of an encouraging word he might give the Plenteys. To Simon he said, "The church is splendid; I know how hard thou hast worked as churchwarden. We owe thee and the others so much."

"Thank thee, old friend. God has been good to us. The effort made by so many seems to be renewing the community of the church. That will last long after we are gone, just as the stones and timbers will."

Lydia had been speaking to Mrs Plentey and now caught up with Ellen as she walked down the path. "I wonder where Isabel will be keeping Easter," she said. "She may be still at Burford."

"When didst thou last hear from her?"

"Four days ago. George had just deserted his father-in-law and been reconciled with his brother, so Isabel's not on our side any more. George of Clarence's four thousand men will march with King Edward."

"And Anne?"

"Still in Normandy waiting for a fair wind. She may be aboard ship by now."

Richard and Simon had reached the market place and before going each to his home for dinner, Simon said, "Thou and I may have a testing time to come, Richard. I fear King Edward is now in a very strong position."

"Yes, I wake in the night, sweating, wondering how I got so caught up in Warwick's affairs. I try telling myself that Warwick, Somerset and Jasper Tudor working together could be unstoppable. But it's not clear who's in charge."

"The Yorkists have one great advantage," said Simon, "a strong king, whose orders are obeyed."

Chapter 26
EASTER MONDAY

On Easter Monday, the fifteenth of April, Mr Plentey had just returned from his visiting and Mrs Plentey had just finished her household duties for the day when they heard a commotion in the yard; a sound of horse's hooves and shouting.

Mrs Plentey thought she recognised Hugh's voice.

"Andrew! Take my horse! He's had a rough journey." They both hurried to the door. Hugh looked dishevelled and distraught. He came towards them.

"Father, hullo! Oh, Mother!"

Mrs Plentey took his hand. "Hugh! Art thou all right? Come in, lad, I'll bring thee some ale." She bustled off to the kitchen.

Mr Plentey looked at his son. "Hugh! Thank God thou'rt safe. Come in boy."

"Father... Warwick's dead, Father. I saw him killed."

"God have mercy on his soul." Plentey crossed himself.

"It was horrible. I saw this fellow, determined to kill him. I could do nothing for him. King Edward's army seemed to be everywhere. There was so much confusion... some of our own men were attacking us. By then we were in flight. Warwick nearly reached his horse in time. He couldn't run in full armour."

Mrs Plentey came in with a cup of ale.

"Anyway, he was exhausted. Before he could mount he was stabbed in the face. My poor Lord of Warwick."

"God rest his soul," Mrs Plentey said. "Drink this,

Hugh."

Hugh took the cup from her and with his other hand held fast to hers for a few moments. He drank and continued more calmly, "The army dispersed. I couldn't see any of the other fellows I'd been with at the start. No more orders were given so I rode away; just pointed westward. I rode about twenty miles, then slept in a barn. The farmer gave me feed for the horse, his wife brought me bread and ale. I rode on today. I could think of nothing, except getting home. Perhaps I should have looked for the others. I just felt numb."

His father said quietly, "The Lancastrians haven't a hope without Warwick. You saw no-one who knew where Robert might be?"

"I saw no-one I knew, apart from the few comrades I was with as the battle was beginning."

"Where was the battle, Hugh?" his mother asked.

"At Barnet. It's near London. The king wanted to prevent our army from entering London. It was on our way as we marched from Coventry. He must have succeeded. Yesterday was Easter Day. We hadn't expected to fight on Easter Day."

"And there was I, thinking of the king celebrating Easter with his family," Mrs Plentey said.

"There was a thick mist in the early morning. It was impossible to tell who was winning. We had the bigger army. We would have won easily without the fog. I don't really know what happened in the end. Except that my Lord of Warwick is dead. Perhaps I should go back."

"Stay a day or two, Hugh," Mrs Plentey said. "Get some rest. There'll be no more fighting this week. Come with me, I'll find thee some food." She made for the door, saying over her shoulder, "When Queen Marguerite lands and hears the news, I should think she'll go straight back to France."

"Thy mother may be right," John Plentey said, "but that'd mean more trouble at a later date."

He hoped profoundly that the queen could be defeated at the earliest possible moment. Surely that was the only way England's turmoil could be concluded.

Hugh followed his mother to the kitchen. John sat quietly for a while, giving thanks for Hugh's safety and praying that Robert too was safe.

It took only an hour or so for the news to become the main topic in the market place. Tim burst in to tell Richard Woolman and he at once sought Lydia, who went round to see the Plenteys. No-one had dreamt that while all of them had been focused on the Easter service such terrible carnage could be taking place.

Lydia returned to hear that one of the pigeons had flown in. Richard showed her the brief message.

"It just says, 'Easter Day' in Latin. Pascha Dies. So the queen has landed at Weymouth. It was to be in French for Dartmouth, English for Portsmouth. Then next: Q,P,A, the assurance that the queen, the prince and Anne are all together. Then a large number to tell how many men were with them."

Chapter 27
A TESTING TIME

Warwick's death changed everything. His naked body and that of his brother Montagu were displayed outside St Paul's Cathedral in London for all to see.

The news had a numbing effect on Richard Woolman at first. He found he was losing interest in the outcome of the struggle. If only life could return to normal, with no anxiety about shipping wool, no looking out for suspicious behaviour, no need for his pigeons to be in the service of Sir Gilbert.

Among the townspeople there was a renewed interest in following the latest turn of events. For long months the struggle had been nothing to do with daily life; there had been no general sense of danger. But all were aware now that the final reckoning was still to come and it could be soon and it was uncertain where it would be.

Lydia could think only of Isabel, Anne and their mother. She could not burden her father with her anguish, and found it impossible to confide even in Ellen. Margery realised she was not herself and spoke kindly to her about loss. Lydia asked her if she still had parents alive. Margery told her she had not and then, after hesitating a while, spoke of a young husband who, sixteen years ago, went bravely off to St Albans to fight for King Harry and never returned.

A short letter arrived from Isabel in London. She had sent a servant round to Adam Fry's headquarters in the City and not many days later he had found an acquaintance about to travel to Gloucester who was prepared to stop with the letter in Northleach. Isabel supposed that her mother and Anne must have heard of her father's death and be overwhelmed with grief. She knew nothing more than the fact that they had arrived in England. Isabel was at present in the Tower. Queen Elizabeth would have nothing to do with her. She could often see the little princesses from her window, out on the green, with their nursemaids. She would have loved to join them in their games but was afraid of upsetting the queen. She was lost and lonely with no household of her own and only infrequent appearances of her husband who was required to stay close to the king.

'I know I must be calm and trust the Lord,' Isabel wrote. 'I'm getting a little better at it. Surely it will all be over before long.'

Lydia was relieved when a pigeon arrived with a message from Anne. Queen Marguerite and her party had marched as far as Cerne Abbey. Lydia was reassured that Anne had her code book safe.

The Vicar had news from Gloucester Abbey that preparations were in hand in case of a battle taking place there. It was difficult to gauge how much support there was for the queen; she and King Harry had been sure of a good welcome in Gloucester in past years but since Warwick's death and Clarence's defection many people thought King Edward likely to triumph. More than anything it was best to be on the winning side. They were accustomed to Edward's good governance and had no reason to rise against him.

Hugh had told Richard Woolman that many of his comrades who had seen Warwick as their hero, were inclined to change sides now that he was dead. The huge contingent of men raised by George of Clarence in the West Country for the Lancastrian army was now with King Edward. Hugh had lain awake at night wondering whether loyalty to a dead leader was more important than taking a detached view of what might be the best outcome for England, for the people, for the wool trade. Suppose King Edward, his brothers and his faithful lords were killed in the next battle? Could England be ruled by a boy king acting for a witless father and influenced by his ruthless mother, the Duke of Somerset and Jasper Tudor?

Rupert told Tom he had heard from a friend in Windsor that the king was there, and many men were rallying to his cause. They discussed the prospects for the next battle.

The labourers had their own discussions. They were shovelling up rubbish; stone chippings, odds and ends of wood and general dirt. Cuthbert was restless.

"I don't know why I keep on with this confounded work. It's hard and dirty, everyone picks on me and the pay's no good," he said.

"Ye could go fer a soldier," Jack suggested.

"That's a mug's game. There may be a better time coming when the goddam fightin's finished and I intend to be alive. Lad I knew in King Henry's army never got paid fer months anyway."

"Couldn't ye be an army cook? Or one of those fellers who scrounge food fer the boys?"

"Nah... tell yer what, though. They pay well fer gravediggers after a battle. Specially in warm weather. What we need is a thunderin' big battle somewhere near here, and there'd be two or three week's fartin' work burying bodies. Bits o' horse as well, after the butchers've finished. Usually perks there too."

Jack shuddered. "I'd rather go on shovelling this lot up than burying stinking bodies. What they all killing each other fer, anyway?"

"Search me. It's a goddam stupid way to settle an argument. Yes, hundred years ago, people didn't know any better. And there were all those fartin' wolves to clear up afterwards. Must be a better way by now."

"What - the wolves ate up the bodies?"

"Yah... and English fellers were fighting blastin' Scots or Frenchies then. 'Taint natural to be killing yer own kind."

"How do the lads know which side to fight on?"

"If they've any sense they'll stay wi' King Edward. Harry's no good as king."

"If I was one of Warwick's men I'd change sides now he's dead."

Cuthbert looked at Jack contemptuously and spat on the floor. "I think *that* of a man who changes sides."

Chapter 28
OVERHEARING

One afternoon when Lydia was walking home past the churchyard she heard voices though she could see no-one. She realised that the sound was coming through the dry-stone wall from a lean-to shed where some of the building materials were stored. A man said, "Hey Rupert! You worked for King Edward. D'you suppose he'd pay me for a message I found?"

"Oh! Where did you find it? Why should the king want it?"

"I picked up a dead pigeon under the hedge. It was still warm; its wing was broken. Thought it might be one of Mr Woolman's. Sure enough, found a flaming message on its leg."

"Let's see." A pause. "I can't puzzle it out."

"Well I can't read. P'raps Woolman's expectin' some news. He is Earl of Warwick's man, ye know?"

"I'll pay you to keep quiet about it. Can you do that?"

"You against Earl of Warwick's people then?"

"Yes. And I'll pay you to keep quiet about that too." He paused. "I think this may be Welsh. Are there any Welshmen in Northleach? Someone who could read?"

"Can't think of anyone. Yes! There's a fellow in Eastington with a Welsh wife. But I don't suppose she can read."

The voices became more muffled and Lydia could make out very few words. Something about changing sides and then the word 'pie'. She realised that the speakers must have turned their backs to her. She hurried home, distraught.

"Lydia! What's upset thee?" her father asked.

"I've just walked past the churchyard. Thou know'st that hut where the men store materials? It's just a lean-to against a dry-stone wall. I discovered long ago that you can hear every word through that wall."

"Well...?"

"That mason, Rupert, was in there with one of the labourers. I think the one called Cuthbert. Cuthbert had picked up a dead pigeon with a message."

"I was expecting one from Bruges, or it might be another from Anne Neville."

"No, it wasn't from Bruges. Rupert thought the writing might be Welsh. He asked Cuthbert if there was a Welshman in Northleach who could read."

"From my Lord Jasper! Don't worry, he's sure to have sent a horseman as well, to be on the safe side. We'll get the news tomorrow."

"But Father! the poor bird has ended up in a pie!"

"After flying so bravely. And so nearly home." He thought for a moment. "I'll ask Joshua which bird is missing; he'll remember which went to Calais and which to Will Skinner." He paused again. "Rupert is King Edward's man. He may be suspicious of me, now. But he's a fine mason."

"Yes, he is suspicious. Cuthbert said, 'Woolman is the Earl of Warwick's man'. Rupert paid Cuthbert to keep quiet. I think we could be in danger from him."

"I wonder how much he knows? We've been so careful."

Lydia looked tearful. "Oh, Father!"

He took her gently by the shoulders. "Come now, where's my brave girl?"

Lydia wiped her eyes and sniffed. "I keep thinking of Isabel and Anne grieving for their father. I thought I could be brave but now I'm fearful for thee."

"It was upsetting for thee, overhearing Rupert."

Lydia continued more calmly, "We were so happy

and inspired in church on Sunday. And then when the pigeon brought the message, I was excited that the queen had landed. But to think my Lord of Warwick was killed the same day. Isabel will feel so alone. And think of Anne and the countess hearing the news the moment they reached England. At least they have each other."

"No, my dear, that's not so. The Portsmouth pigeon has arrived. The message gives the number of men landed and adds that the Countess of Warwick was aboard. We know Anne was with the queen."

Chapter 29
PREPARATIONS

Lydia showed Ellen a letter she had received from Isabel. Lydia watched as Ellen realised suddenly that it was quite easy to read as Lydia had transcribed it. She read it aloud to Lydia.

"It's dated 22nd April, only three days ago.

> I'm at Windsor with my husband for the Feast of St George and the Garter Ceremony. The king and his army will march west soon and I have to go back to the Tower of London for safety. I have heard nothing from my mother or Anne. When you write, please tell them I pray for them every day.
> Thank thee for thy note about Father. I still feel numb. If I try to think, I'm overcome with sadness that I can do nothing for Mother.
> The king is in high spirits; he saw his baby son for the first time just before Easter. He keeps George close to him at all times; I can understand why. Their brother, Richard, is free to come and go. He has proved his loyalty again and again. King Edward spoke kindly to me; I know he is genuinely sorry at Father's death. One of my servants rides to London today and has promised to go to your cousin's house with this letter. I shall not be able to write to you again. I pray for your safety, Lydia, and for your dear ones. Isabel."

"It sounds a bit stiff, translated from code," Lydia explained.

"I shouldn't like to be sent to the Tower by the king,"

"No, it sounds ominous, doesn't it? But it's the safest place in London, well defended and well provisioned. The queen will go back there to her children. King Henry is there too. Poor King Harry - Cousin Fry said that he was taken to Barnet and kept under guard just behind the battle lines for fear he might be recaptured by the Lancastrians."

"Dost thou know where Hugh is?"

"No. Some of our men have been sent to Bristol. Hugh may be with them. Father says they have to wait for a decision whether to march to London or to Worcester. The queen will probably do one or the other and the king will have to decide where to intercept her."

"My father said he heard another lot marching on the Fosse early this morning."

The next morning, when Lydia came in with bread from the bakery, she told her father, "They're saying in the market place that Rupert the mason has bribed Mr Plentey's stable boy and taken his best horse to ride to Gloucester with an important message for King Edward's men."

"I wonder what he knows? I suppose I should have asked Skinner's men to watch him." He felt uneasy about this.

A few days later Ellen and her father came round to Woolman's house in the evening as they often did now the days were warmer. The two girls always had plenty of needlework to do. They mended clothes while the light lasted and then took up their knitting which could be done mostly by feel.

Tonight, they found themselves listening to their fathers' conversation. Richard told Simon that the queen and her army had reached Bristol. There was strong support there. Heavy guns had been assembled with oxen to pull them.

"Will told me there's disagreement between the Duke of Somerset and the Earl of Devon as to the way to take next," Richard said. "Most townspeople between Weymouth and Bristol favour the Lancastrians but many places have their factions now, specially since so many West Country men marched with George of Clarence and switched sides to join King Edward."

"And what will Warwick's men do? Who is leading them now?"

"It's hard to know. Lord Oxford has disappeared, presumably fled abroad. Exeter was severely wounded. Somerset and Devon were not present at Barnet, nor were Lord Wenlock and Jasper Tudor."

"Dost thou think Jasper will bring his Welsh Army to England through Gloucester?" Simon asked.

"It's possible. King Harry always used to get a good reception in Gloucester, but I don't know whether the people would favour Queen Marguerite now. She has had such a terrible reputation since her army marched through England killing and looting ten years ago."

"Jasper wouldn't leave Wales unless he was sure the queen was bound for London, would he? He'd prefer the queen to meet him at Gloucester or Worcester, before deciding on their next move."

"Thou'rt right." Richard paused. "I suppose most townspeople hope the battle will be somewhere else. I doubt if either army would get much of a welcome in Northleach."

The following day a pigeon arrived with a message from Anne. Lydia translated it from code. Anne said that the queen had changed her mind and was trying to persuade Jasper to use the ships at Bristol to bring *his* army across the Severn to join hers. Richard was puzzled by this, until shortly after, when a horseman brought a letter from Will Skinner and

he realised that the pigeon had overtaken the horse.
Will wrote:

> There are ships ready in Bristol to take our
> whole army and equipment across the
> River Severn to Chepstow. Jasper Tudor
> has come over by ferry to persuade the
> queen that this is the best course of
> action. The queen has agreed. We are
> surprised by this as she has always said
> she would stay on dry land whatever
> happened.

Later, Richard thought this over. He wondered to
himself how long the queen and her lords would wait
for Jasper to make up his mind. Had they been told
how many men had arrived so far in Chepstow? Will
had told him he had his own suspicion that Jasper
was more interested in keeping his Welshmen safe
than supporting Queen Marguerite.

"Keep that to yourself, sir," Will had said. "When
Jasper visited London, he was impressed by
Warwick's care of King Henry and felt that his
intention to give wise guidance to young Prince
Edouard, when Edward of York had been defeated,
was genuine."

But Warwick's death had changed all that.

Chapter 30
THE VICAR'S HOSPITALITY

The Vicar invited his colleagues from Farmington, Hampnett, Turkdean and Yanworth to a special meal at his house on the first of May. He had been making preparations for over a week. The day dawned clear and warm but a shadow hung over it as they all knew that a great battle would take place soon. The three women who took turns caring for Geoffrey Langbroke and his house excelled themselves cooking tempting dishes; the men enjoyed sharing the meal.

Conversation ranged widely; for a while no-one talked of the impending battle. It was in all their minds and at last Geoffrey spoke of the decision that the French queen and her advisers needed to make: whether to march to London or Gloucester. The mighty River Severn still divided the queen's army from that of Jasper Tudor. Geoffrey described the river. As a boy he had ridden once with his father to Tewkesbury and returned to Gloucester by boat. The boatman had told the boy he would wait for the tide to turn and then be swept back to Tewkesbury.

The men questioned Geoffrey about the queen's hope of crossing into Wales if Gloucester's gates were closed to her. He told them of the skilled ferrymen who made the crossing at Tewkesbury even when the water was high after the snows melted on the Welsh mountains.

"If an army was to be ferried across the river at Tewkesbury, they would need to start at first light and even then they might not all get across in one day," he explained. "When the water is not at its highest the river can be forded at low tide. But even using the ford, they would need a start of at least two days to be sure of getting a whole army, with guns and baggage, across.

"The vale is so beautiful in early May," he told them. "The may blossom will be fully out now. If you walk only a few yards from Gloucester there are flowers everywhere."

Around Northleach the may was budding, bright new leaves only just beginning to unfurl on beech and elm, the ash trees still showing their winter tracery.

They talked then of the horror of the impending battle. Christian Englishmen would soon be butchering each other. Geoffrey told them of the two Plentey brothers serving on opposing sides. The Vicar of Farmington had heard of another family stricken in the same way.

After his friends had left, Geoffrey's thoughts went back to a few days earlier when Hugh Plentey had come to him in great turmoil of mind after witnessing the horrors of the Battle of Barnet. He had seen worthy English citizens hacking each other to death with terrible ferocity. The cries of injured men and the patient agony of horses had torn his heart. He was worried that he had behaved in a cowardly way because he had shrunk from the brutality; the stories he had heard before, glorified war.

"I have witnessed such terrible things, Sir Geoffrey," Hugh had said. "I didn't know how beastly a battle would be. Men you would normally be pleased to meet, charging at each other with loud shrieks, wielding battleaxes. I found it difficult to imitate them."

Geoffrey had recognised the plight of the inexperienced soldier. There was nothing he could say but Hugh needed him only to listen.

"I can't tell any of my friends and family about it,

sir. I hope you don't mind my bringing it to you."

Geoffrey had reassured him and told him it was always so. But this carnage in England was extra difficult. It was easier to imagine a foreigner as your enemy.

Hugh agreed. "Sir, I have even felt unsure which side to fight on next time. It sounds so disloyal, but after Barnet I thought of deserting the Lancastrian army as so many others have done. My hero was my Lord of Warwick. Without him the fight seems meaningless.

"At Barnet I knew my brother was on the other side. I prayed desperately I would not see him on the battlefield. I did not and I was very relieved when my father heard he was safe. When we come to the next battle perhaps I should be with Robert. I know my father thinks so. Or I could just go back to Calais; there must be plenty of work waiting for me there. But what would my Lord of Warwick think of that? He had thrown in his lot with Queen Marguerite and the young prince and their kinsmen."

The Vicar had then prayed aloud and hoped the words would calm Hugh.

They had sat quietly together a little longer. Then Hugh had thanked him and said he felt sure now he should not change sides.

Geoffrey had heard the next morning that Hugh had left for Bristol.

Chapter 31
ELLEN READS A NOTICE

Richard Woolman was in the counting house, checking his notes for Will Skinner. He was weighed down by the feeling that nothing he had done had helped to further Warwick's cause. Of course, he couldn't see the whole picture and Will had assured him his help was important, but he didn't really believe him.

He sometimes wondered whether King Edward had spies in Northleach watching *him*. He knew that Tim enjoyed the gossip of the market place and had warned him to keep his mouth shut; Will had been careful to visit only after dark. Richard thought back to the evening when, thanks to his pigeon, he had been the first to know of the queen's arrival at Weymouth. That message had been intended for the Earl of Warwick, who had died that day. Richard had felt unable to ask Joshua to take the message to Bibury; he had had several nights out recently, tending lambing ewes. Instead, Tim had been summoned. Could there be a man out there watching Woolman's house for unusual events?

Tim had just had time to ride to the inn at Bibury before dusk. Richard knew the people at one of the farms on the Saltway and had told Tim to ask for a night's lodging there. It was not safe for a young boy to be out alone in the dark, particularly in the narrow lane that turned off the Saltway for Northleach.

Richard turned again to the notes he was writing for Will Skinner, to make sure he had left nothing out, but he wasn't going to get a moment's peace. Someone was calling outside. He heard Lydia hurry to the door.

Lydia had recognised Ellen's voice but she had never heard her shouting in excitement before. She opened the door and Ellen burst in.

"Lyddie!" Ellen began. "Oh, excuse me, Mr Woolman. I've been to Cirencester with Father. I've something important to tell you."

"Ellen! Whatever's happened?" said Lydia.

"Father had to see a man in Castle Street on business. He took him into his inner room and asked me to wait. I walked across the room to look out of the window. There was a paper lying on the table; it looked easy to read. I had read it before I realised how wrong it was to pry into someone's business! The writing was quite large and I was pleased with myself: I could follow the words without saying them aloud, like thou taught'st me last week."

"Well done! What was this private business?"

"It seemed to be a message for King Edward's men. It said that Queen Marguerite's army is in Bristol and prepares to march to London while making a pretence it goes instead to Gloucester."

"King Edward's men have already marched south from Cirencester," said Richard. "The king would certainly prefer to fight before the Welsh arrive. You'll keep this to yourself, Ellen, my dear."

"Of course, Mr Woolman."

"Is there anything else we can do?" Lydia said.

"I'll pass on your information, Ellen. Then we can only watch and wait."

As they left the room, Ellen told Lydia that Mrs Plentey had said that Mr Plentey had asked for the church bells to be rung when the battle was over. The bass bell for King Henry or all the bells for King Edward.

Richard decided he would take Ellen's message to Bibury, himself. On the way back he could call at the farm on the Saltway to thank his friend for his kindness to Tim.

The next day another message came from Will

Skinner. Plans had changed again. It appeared that Jasper had not yet mustered all his Welshmen.

It was now clear that the Welsh would not be crossing the Severn to join the queen at Bristol. The queen's army would march for Gloucester, not London, and hope to meet Jasper's men there. The Duke of Somerset had heard that King Edward was camped near Sodbury Hill. The duke had sent a small force to pretend to take up battle positions one evening and leave during the night to join the march of the main army towards Gloucester.

King Edward's men were deceived for a few hours but not delayed long. The king decided to march north-east over the hilltops and try to overtake the queen's army in the valley bottom. So they were making for Gloucester after all.

Will Skinner came himself, late on the next day. He hoped for news of the Welsh army; he thought Richard Woolman might have had a message by pigeon. Will said that Somerset had lost touch with Jasper. The queen's army had reached Berkeley.

The queen was losing patience with Jasper. Will didn't think she realised that the Welsh still felt sore that so many of their archers had died defending Edward from Warwick's army at Edgecote, in spite of the fact that it was Edward, before he was king, who had had Jasper's father beheaded in Hereford market place. Many were wary of getting involved again.

Will had ridden from Berkeley and was exhausted. Woolman could give him no news but could offer food and a place to sleep. He was gone again at dawn.

Chapter 32
THE BATTLE

By the third of May Richard Woolman knew that King Edward's men had prevented Queen Marguerite from entering Gloucester. The king's main army was still in the hills, about level with the queen's in the valley. It seemed that the queen hoped to reach the bridge at Upton or possibly Worcester, to cross into Wales. This was now looking unlikely.

If she could not reach one of the bridges, then the fourth of May would be the day of the battle. Richard was on edge all day. Simon came round in the evening to sit with him while they waited for news.

"I'll go up to bed, Father," said Lydia. "I can't keep awake. We'll surely hear first thing in the morning."

"Good night, my dear. I'll stay up; I'm sure I wouldn't sleep."

"Shall I get thee another drink?"

"No thanks. I can get more for Simon and me later on. Thou go on up."

The men sat on quietly for a while, then Simon asked if Richard would tell him exactly what he had heard. Richard said, "Will Skinner was here late Thursday night: that's forty-eight hours ago. Told me he'd ridden from Berkeley. The queen's army was having a few hours rest there and was to march again at midnight. For Gloucester."

"So it was yesterday that thou heard'st that Gloucester city gates were closed to the queen."

"Yes, a Welsh lad came with news; he had crossed the Severn by ferry. He said most of Jasper's men were halfway between Chepstow and Newnham."

"So they're too late."

"Yes. Sir Richard Beauchamp had enough men to hold the south gate for King Edward. He's governor of the city and castle. We have hundreds of supporters in Gloucester but they could not overcome the guards in time. The queen had no choice but to march on towards Tewkesbury.

"Will Skinner came again late last night. He'd been to Cheltenham. King Edward's army reached there at five o'clock and rested before marching on to Twyning to camp. They had travelled over the hills from Sodbury to Birdlip all in one day while the Lancastrians marched through the vale. A messenger had sought Will out to say the queen's army was camped at Tewkesbury, this side of the river."

"It was a hot day; they must all have been exhausted." After musing for a few minutes, Simon went on, "What about the message that Rupert found on the injured pigeon?"

"People seem to think it was in Welsh and that he was going to Gloucester hoping to find a Welshman."

"If he was a spy, he was rather a careless one!"

"Will asked me last week if I'd seen anyone acting suspiciously. I'm ashamed now that I didn't tell him about Rupert. I was a coward, Simon. I thought Will's men might kill Rupert. I couldn't face it; he's a fine mason."

"Thou would'st have tormented thyself if he'd died on account of thy information. But I think it's unlikely Rupert could have made any difference." Simon was unconvinced that Rupert was a serious threat.

"Thou'rt probably right."

"How soon will we get news, think'st thou?" Simon asked after a pause.

"Tim's ridden to the inn at Andoversford hoping to hear something. But he'll not start for home before daybreak."

"The battle must have been over some hours

now. A rider direct from Tewkesbury could be here soon."

They sat on, until at last Simon said, "I must be getting home."

Richard rose to his feet. "Stay for another drink, Simon."

But Simon rose too and started for the door. "Thanks, but I must get a little sleep. Folks will expect their bread as usual."

"Thou'll be glad of the work. I can't concentrate on any of mine."

"That's the good thing about baking. I can relieve my frustration kneading the dough. Thanks for thy hospitality, Richard."

As his friend opened the door Simon heard the sound they had waited for.

"The bell, Richard."

Then the whole peal sounded. "All the bells, Simon. Victory for King Edward."

Chapter 33
BACK TO NORMAL

Tom went early to the church as usual, on the Monday after the Battle of Tewkesbury. There were no flowers and altar cloths now, sheets covered the figures of the saints, but it had not altogether reverted to a building site. There were lighted candles in the chancel where the Vicar was kneeling for his morning prayers. Tom walked round the north aisle quietly, making a few notes.

The Vicar rose and crossed himself. He saw Tom and called out, "It's a beautiful morning, Tom. Good day to you."

"Good day to you, sir." The two men met in the nave.

"We have much to be thankful for. That includes your work, Tom."

"Yes, sir. I give thanks daily we have been able to finish so much of it. And that Northleach has been spared from battles. Sir Geoffrey, I heard that Robert Plentey was killed. God rest his soul. Was he the only Northleach man to be lost?"

"Yes, I believe so. Hugh is safe, though not home yet. I am praying for the Plenteys."

"Such a terrible price has been paid. Let's hope there'll be no more trouble."

After a pause, the Vicar said, "Now Tom, have you any craftsmen still or did they all leave to fight?"

"Sir, Rupert has disappeared without a word and without last week's pay!"

"I heard he was in the king's service and might return to Windsor."

"But he told me he intended to stay to finish carving the last two figures."

"And have you any labourers? It seems very quiet."

"Cuthbert left suddenly. Said he could find work in Tewkesbury. I've had a couple of lads from the Earl of Warwick's army asking for work. They're starting tomorrow."

The tower door opened and Joshua came in. "Good morning, sir, morning Tom."

"Have you news, Joshua?" Sir Geoffrey asked.

"Yes sir, my wife has been delivered of a baby girl. A bonny lass. Now Tom, I've escaped from all the bustle at home. What would you have me do next?"

"It's a happy day for you, Joshua," Geoffrey said. "I know we are all thankful to God for your wife's safety. I must leave now, for my morning visits, Tom."

"Will you greet Mr and Mrs Plentey for me, sir?"

"I will Tom, God be with you both."

"And with you, Sir Geoffrey," they said.

Tom turned to Joshua. "I'm truly happy for you, my lad. Now there's something that needs to be done over here in the north aisle."

Two days later, Lydia received a letter from Anne Neville. Her relief was great. She had agonised over Anne every day, trying to imagine what she must be going through, how she would be coping with so many troubles.

She shared it at once with Ellen who was glad for her friend to have heard at last.

"Dearest Lydia, I'm at Coventry Abbey. All the servants here know Mother, and are making a great fuss of me. I was brought here with Queen Marguerite and her ladies. We had to line up in the Guildhall in front of King Edward. The king was kind. He took my hand for a moment and said I would be sent to London into George and Isabel's care when things had quietened down there. He marched to

London then. Queen Marguerite travelled there too, as a prisoner.

Oh Lyddie! I'm sure you know that Father is dead - and my poor young prince. We saw some of the men fleeing from the battle. It was horrible. I even feel sorry for the queen. She is grieving for her son and I'm sure will not be allowed to see her husband when she gets to London. She was seasick when we crossed the Channel from Normandy. The wind kept changing and we were twenty days at sea. I haven't seen Mother. The queen ordered her to sail in a different ship. I've heard only that she's safe at Beaulieu. I know Esther and Faith were with her on the same ship. I hope all is well with you and your dear ones. God bless you, Lyddie. Please write, Anne.

There's a bit in code at the end. I think she wants me to know she has the code book safe,

I believe the king has real regret that Father was killed. I wish Mother, Isabel and I could all be together. It's hard, grieving by myself. The best of all would be to come to thee for comfort, Lyddie. I do want to see Isabel but I feel uneasy with George.

I long to go to her. Coventry is not so far."

"It's not possible, is it Lyddie?"

"No, just a daydream. Father needs me here."

"Thou must be here when Hugh comes back, Lyddie! Dost thou think Mrs Plentey would like us to visit her together?"

That evening, a cart arrived from Tewkesbury. Robert's body had been found and loaded at the last minute with others bound for Oxford. John Plentey sent a man to Tewkesbury to look for Hugh and tell him to come home for the funeral. Hugh had seen King Edward's officers searching the bodies of their fallen comrades for identity papers. He, with two other men who had escaped injury, had begun to do the same for the Lancastrians. They had not had much success.

Hugh felt compelled to return to Tewkesbury after Robert's funeral, knowing how much it had meant to his father and mother that Robert's body had been found. The work became more and more grim, given the warm weather and the sickening stench. The gravediggers were working across the field and getting closer. Late in the afternoon, Hugh and his two friends agreed they could do no more. He walked for an hour by the River Severn to calm his mind then ordered a meal at The Black Bear Inn where he had left his horse. He found a bed there too; exhaustion ensured that he at last had a complete night's sleep.

Hugh started for home early the next morning. The main road was busy so he decided to travel cross-country to Winchcombe and climb the escarpment on the rough track behind Sudeley Castle. The path was steep and not safe for a descent, but Hugh had been up it before and knew how to tackle it. He dismounted for the steepest stretch; it was better for man and horse each to pick a way carefully. Before reaching the top, Hugh paused for breath and turned to look back. The sun shone on the peaceful valley. He shuddered at the thought of what had happened down in Severn Vale just beyond those quiet hills.

Reaching the top, Hugh mounted his horse and turned right on to the Saltway, which would cross the Gloucester Road close to Northleach.

The Fosseway was busy but Northleach seemed quiet.

It was the day of Stow Horse Fair. A party of men

had gone from Northleach, mainly to find horses and mules for the wool train. Prices were likely to be high after the loss of so many horses on the battlefield of Tewkesbury. Joshua was one of the party; Richard Woolman knew he was likely to find the right sort of animals to carry the woolpacks. Mr Plentey sent a man he knew to be a good judge of a horse to find him a replacement for the one that was stolen. Tim was sent too, to mind the men's own horses while they went into the town. Joshua knew a good place close to Stow where they could tie their mounts to a stout fence in the shade of a beech tree. Tim was told when to water them and not to take his eyes off them all day. Tim had company enough with many other lads having been given the same duties.

Chapter 34
HUGH'S RETURN

As on most fine days, Lydia was out walking. The grass was growing well, nettles grew by the walls; the may was fully out, covering the bushes with gleaming white curds that seemed about to pour into a milkmaid's pail. It would soon be time to shear the sheep.

A cuckoo called from across the valley. She leant on a gate near the top of the hill, glorying in nature's profusion. She heard a cheery whistle and turned to see Hugh coming up the hill towards her. She ran to him and he caught her in his arms.

"I thought I might find you here," he said and held her at arm's length to have a good look.

"Hugh! When did you get back?"

"Two minutes ago. No, I had to see Mother and Father first."

She thought then of Robert. She freed her hands. "Your poor family. Such a relief you're safe, but such grief for Robert. You're quite unharmed, Hugh?"

"I was fortunate. I saw men with terrible injuries. I stayed to do what I could for them. It wasn't much. It's a sad time. All our hopes of victory are dashed. I needed badly to see you."

He hugged then released her. "Have you heard from the Nevilles?"

"Anne is safe, in Coventry Abbey. A widow at fifteen. And the countess widowed too. I haven't heard from Isabel."

"She must be in London."

"Yes. The countess has taken refuge with the

Cistercian Sisters at Beaulieu. It's near Southampton. And your parents, Hugh? They'll be needing you. You can't fill Robert's place but they'll need to keep you close. King Edward's victory was what they wanted - but at what a cost."

"I need to keep thee close, Lyddie. I've been wanting to tell thee. I love thee, Lydia. Could'st thou love me?"

"Oh Hugh, I've so longed to see thee. I love thee more than anyone in the world!"

"Wilt thou marry me, Lyddie?"

"Yes, Hugh. Tomorrow if thou lik'st!"

"Dost thou think thy father would allow me to court thee?"

Lydia laughed at Hugh's sudden change to formality. "Please ask him Hugh. He's very upset about my Lord of Warwick. This might cheer him."

Hugh kissed her then and all conversation was suspended. He freed her at last and breathlessly she said, "Wilt thou have to go back to Calais?"

"I don't know what Father has in mind. He told me the wool train has not left because there are no ships ready."

"Yes, my father is anxious too about shifting last year's wool before shearing begins."

They started back towards the town. "Wilt thou meet me up here, Lyddie, this time tomorrow? It'll give me a day to judge whether Mother is ready for this. She's fond of thee, Lyddie. She'll be happy for us. But I must speak to thy father first."

Lydia giggled to herself as she went up to bed that night. She thought of her younger self, at Middleham, looking round the Great Hall at the young men, handsome and otherwise. Hugh was not tall and dark, but of medium height with light brown hair and grey eyes. Certainly they were smiling eyes.

Chapter 35
TEWKESBURY DEATH TOLL

In the following days, Richard Woolman was busy with his affairs. There was still some unrest in London. He had tried to find men to take his pigeons to various Kent ports for news of ships ready to sail but there seemed to be few reliable messengers. Simon Trencher came round to see him.

"I didn't come yesterday," he said, "as I knew thou hadst thy cousin Fry with thee. Is all well with him?"

"He's well, thank thee. Didst hear that he brought news of King Harry's death in the Tower of London?"

"I hadn't heard. God rest his soul." Simon crossed himself. "He's earned his rest, but he should not have died in the Tower."

Richard looked through the papers on his desk. "Adam brought this little tribute to the old king." He passed it to Simon.

Simon read it over and said, "I like this: 'King Henry the Sixth was venerated for his humility, tenderness and approachability'." He paused, then said, "Such a good man; so ill-used; so unfit for kingship."

Richard went towards the door. "Come into the garden, Simon. I've had enough of the counting house for this morning." He led the way. The sun was warm outside, the birds were singing and the apple tree was resplendent in white blossom. The old dog lay on his side in its shade and flicked his tail lazily in greeting.

"King Edward has had no peace since the battle. Adam said he went on to Coventry to put down riots there. At the same time there was a rebel attack on London. Adam was in no hurry to travel until this week when London was quieter. He was pleased with the wool we showed him but uncertain when it can be shipped. The ships that are usually in the Channel ports have been commandeered by the rebels or by the king, or captured by pirates. He hopes trade will revive in the next few weeks."

"The king will be needing the taxes from the Calais Staple so he'll release some ships as soon as he can."

"Yes, he'll not delay and we must be ready."

Simon was startled when his friend sank on to the bench, his head in his hands. Usually he hid his feelings. "Richard! What's wrong?"

"My cousin brought this as well." He took a paper from his pocket and handed it to Simon who sat down on the bench beside him. "That's a list of the men killed at Tewkesbury. I had a terrible dream last night. I was at Tewkesbury - yet it was not Tewkesbury. I saw the faces of hundreds of doomed men."

"I have grieved and prayed for them," Simon said. "It is a great sacrifice."

"Maybe I could have stopped the mason Rupert from going to Gloucester. The queen's army might have reached Wales in time. If only my Lord Jasper had been with her at Bristol. If only they'd crossed by the Severn Ferry..."

"Richard! Everyone did their best. It wasn't enough. It happens every day." He read through the list and handed the paper back to Richard. He saw Lydia come out from the house. "Lydia! Good morning. We are grieving for the brave men of Tewkesbury." Both men rose to their feet.

"Good morning, Mr Trencher," Lydia said. "I've been telling Father we must look ahead now. Put the battles behind us. At last it is decided who is king. King Edward has usually been just and merciful.

There is nothing to fear."

"I expect you're right, Lydia." Simon replied. "You have your life before you and have hope and courage. I am still anxious for our country. King Harry was the true king and has been treated harshly. His friends won't forget."

"No-one will have the stomach for battles for a long time, Mr Trencher. See if you can rouse Father from his melancholy; I must be about my work." She set off up the garden with her basket, the dog following her. Simon had not heard Lydia speak abruptly before and realised she was being sorely tried just when she was ready to start life anew. He looked at his friend; he had never seen him so shaken before.

Richard was still looking at the list of names with a dazed expression on his face. "I have a need to call their names and see their frightened eyes close," he said, sitting down again.

"They were all brave men, Richard. They didn't fear battle; they feared God. They prayed for an end to strife in England as we all do."

Woolman still couldn't look his friend in the eye. He began to read aloud. It seemed he believed this would help. "Prince Edouard, only son of King Henry the Sixth and Queen Marguerite, aged seventeen. The Duke of Somerset, Sir John Beaufort, Lord Wenlock." He paused. "The Earl of Devon and Sir John Langstrother. Sir Gervase Clifton, Sir Robert Whittingham and Sir Walter Courtenay. Nicholas Hervey, the Recorder of Bristol. Sir Humphrey Bourchier, cousin to King Edward. Countless men whose names are not known. And Robert Plentey." He sighed and put the paper away. "It must never happen again."

"Ellen has been with Lydia to visit Mrs Plentey. She's a brave woman, Richard."

Richard met his eyes at last. "What can I say to John Plentey? I've lost no family. But I have lost my

Lord of Warwick. If only he could have lived, Simon. The earl and his lady did so much for Lydia."

"You stayed loyal to my Lord of Warwick, Richard. Hold on to that."

"He was a fine, brave, generous man. Yet he proved too ambitious."

The next morning Richard discovered that his old dog had died quietly in his sleep.

Chapter 36
THE AFTERMATH

Richard Woolman found Simon Trencher's quiet support helped him through his distress over the loss of the men of Tewkesbury and of his hero, Warwick. More than anything he was cheered by the prospect of a new life for Lydia and Hugh. He settled back into his routine work preparing for the departure of the wool train and the shipping of his wool.

Lydia found her support in Ellen; together they tried to find ways to help the Plentey family. Lydia began to understand Hugh's need sometimes to be alone. How hard it must be for him with no comrade in Northleach who had known battle. She understood that he could not speak of it to her, the memory was so raw and he must be questioning all the time why he had been spared the fate of his brother. Besides, he must ease the load on his mother and father in any way he could, often listening to their reminiscences of the early days of their boys, when he longed to move into the future. He had only a short time with them before he must leave to search the Thames wharves and possibly the Kent ports too, for ships to take the wool to Calais.

Lydia and Hugh had short times alone together. They met in the fields each afternoon, thankful for the tranquil setting of the countryside in spring. They talked of their aspirations for the future, sometimes resting on the grass, holding hands, quietly listening to sheep calls and birdsong.

Lydia could put her own anguish behind her now, that time of anticipation of battle. The sense of

Hugh's danger had nearly overwhelmed her. She was surprised, as she faced his nearing departure for London, that she was no longer afraid for him. Anybody who travelled could fall from a horse or be shipwrecked at sea; fighting was altogether different.

Hugh could not know how vivid in her imagination were the horrors of battle. She had seen many young men at Middleham and overheard some of their conversations and realised only too clearly that they set off to war not only eager to face danger and willing to do their duty but also proud of their skill with deadly weapons; and that they were trained to kill.

In her own sensation of relief she still understood instinctively that for Hugh the reaction must continue to be painful and the memories almost unbearable. Healing would take time.

Indeed for Hugh, waking often in the night in terror, his hope was that getting back to his work in the wool business would restore some sort of normality. Before leaving for London, he again sought out Geoffrey Langbroke, the Vicar, the only man with whom he could share his burden.

He found him on his bench by the river, resting longer than usual in the afternoon after a busy morning. He had baptized two little boys, Peter and Paul, on the previous day; there was a large number of Peters and Pauls in Northleach. He was once again preoccupied with their namesakes. He saw Hugh coming along the path by the river.

He greeted him and was about to speak to him of his parents when he found that Hugh couldn't wait to unburden himself. He told of the horrors he had witnessed at Tewkesbury, even greater than those of Barnet. When the battle was over, the victorious King Edward had ordered that even those who had surrendered or fled the battlefield must be killed. Even when they had sought sanctuary in the Abbey. This was a new ruthless Edward; it was hard to obey him. The young Prince Edouard was amongst those murdered. Hugh had heard that the prince had pleaded for his life to George of Clarence who had so recently sworn his loyalty to him. This had shaken Hugh but he told Geoffrey there could be no rules about mercy in war; it was not a game.

Hugh had not been able to speak before about the ghastly scene on the field after the battle, or of how he had hoped to discover the identity of some of the fallen on the queen's side. Most of them were French soldiers or mercenaries sent by King Louis and there was no possibility of getting the bodies back across the sea.

There was little more need for words. Speaking softly, Geoffrey thanked his Lord that the conflict was over. He told Hugh he prayed daily for his family, patient and dignified in their grief. After they had sat quietly together for a little while. Hugh told Geoffrey he would need to be away next week and the Vicar promised to keep close to his parents.

Geoffrey went out for another round of visits, and later found his mind full of memories of the Plentey boys. In his early days in Northleach he had taught elementary Latin to some of the more studious boys of the parish, in the room over the church porch which, with its hearth and chimney, could be made comfortable in winter. Most of them had lost interest as they grew older and were required to work for their fathers.

He was reaching the point of giving up Latin lessons, when one day the Plentey boys joined his class and, having been told that the wool they saw loaded on the pack-horses was going to London and would need to cross the sea, asked him questions about ships he had seen in Gloucester. They had never seen the sea and knew ships only from pictures.

Geoffrey had looked up St Paul's last voyage when he was taken as a prisoner to Rome. He told Robert and Hugh how the sailors, after being delayed some days by a headwind, had tried to reach a harbour in Crete where they could take cover in good time before the winter storms. Just before they could reach safety, a strong wind had driven them farther out to sea and they suffered the violence of a great storm for two weeks before the ship was wrecked off Malta. He had certainly gained the boys' attention.

"It's all here in Latin," he told them. It was Hugh who asked to see the book and over the next few weeks puzzled over it, asking again and again for help with a particular phrase. He drew pictures of imaginary ships and tried to work out from the text what Paul's ship would have been like. Geoffrey had seen a great many ships in dock but had never been to sea. He could only encourage Hugh to ask any of his father's friends who had been on a wool ship to describe how it was sailed.

Before he left for London, Hugh told Geoffrey that he was courting Lydia Woolman.

Chapter 37
JACK

Tom woke unusually early and decided to get up and start the day. The birds were greeting the dawn and it was not cold. He made a fire in the grate, put a pot of water to boil and went out to gather fresh young nettles for his favourite infusion. Just beyond the cottages he saw three men talking quietly. Two were in King Edward's livery, holding their horses' heads. The third looked like Jack, the labourer. Tom had not seen him for a few days. It looked like Jack and yet somehow not the Jack he knew. This Jack held himself erect and seemed to be speaking fluently, making gestures with his hands, though Tom could not hear the words. The two soldiers mounted and rode away. Jack realised suddenly that he was being watched and came up the lane to speak to Tom.

They greeted each other and Jack said, "I have something to tell you privately Tom."

"I'll be at the church in half an hour." Tom never welcomed people into his home, only too aware how poor and shabby it looked. "The Vicar will not be in for an hour after that. The door may still be locked but I'll be in the porch."

Tom made his hot drink and buttered two slices of bread to eat before going round to the church. Jack was sitting on one of the stone benches in the porch and jumped up when he saw Tom.

"Sit down, lad, I'll be on me feet most of the day so I might as well rest a minute now." Tom sat down on the bench opposite Jack.

"Tom, I deceived you into thinking I was a

labouring man and not a very good one at that. But I am in King Edward's service and was sent here by my superior two years ago when agents were spread across England looking out for trouble from supporters of the Earl of Warwick. I have sharp ears and a good memory." He paused. He saw he had Tom's attention.

"Go on," said Tom.

"A man was needed here because there are two important routes crossing at Northleach and many travellers. For a while I didn't find anything of interest. Then I realised that one of the wool merchants had a particular loyalty to Warwick. His daughter had come back to him after spending time in Warwick's family.

"For a while I just listened to everything I could. I slipped down to the market place at dinner times and on market days stayed a bit longer sweeping the ground behind the stalls - there was always a broom leaning against a post or a table. I kept abreast of all the gossip. I met Tim, Mr Woolman's servant, who also listened to gossip. He was very free with information though surprisingly discreet about Mr Woolman himself. He unintentionally supplied me with several clues. After the Earl of Warwick fled to Normandy I heard of a suspicion that he might have used one of Mr Woolman's pigeons to bring him a message across the Channel. Tim remarked one day that more pigeons than usual were being despatched in baskets, but he didn't know whither they were bound."

"What about Rupert?" Tom asked. "I thought he was in the king's service."

"He is one of the king's masons and fancied himself as something more. He didn't know anything about me. It was I who found the dying pigeon and took the message from its leg. I gave the bird a sharp blow to finish its misery and fastened another piece of paper to its leg; a scrap I found in my pocket. It was a note that was first in English and then in Welsh, ending with a New Year greeting of encouragement. I tore off the bottom bit. I didn't know who might find the bird and moved away as quickly as I could. Rupert guessed the writing was in Welsh so I was the cause of his sudden departure. I am not proud of this - I usually consider the consequences of my actions more carefully. When I got back to my lodgings in the evening I looked at the pigeon's original message and could make neither head nor tail of it. Just a list of numbers. It was probably a code. But I remember that at the end there were two numbers that were written larger; 144, twelve dozen, so very likely a quantity of wool or a price, followed by 145."

They fell silent, Jack still pondering those two numbers which seemed of no particular interest to Tom.

"So Cuthbert had no idea who you were?"

"No. I have a respect for Cuthbert, you know. He had some annoying ways but he was extremely consistent. For him, Cuthbert was number one - but after that everyone was of equal importance, so long as they were English! He treated me fairly and he had a deep contempt for anyone who had made his mind up and then changed sides.

"I was trying to decide what to say to you, Tom. Now that the earl is dead I don't feel I have to deceive you any longer. I am considering leaving the king's service. Perhaps it was a good thing you found me out this morning when I had let my guard down. I was tempted to leave without a word, you know."

"You've certainly given me something to think about, lad! I would never have guessed. I'll keep ye on as labourer if ye'll stay. Had you ever thought of an apprenticeship?"

"I wouldn't make a skilled craftsman, Tom. I'll gladly stay another month, labouring, if you can trust me to be meself!"

"I'm short of men and at least ye know yer way around. I think we'd have to let Joshua know your secret, but best not tell anyone else."

"I'm not sure that'd be fair, Tom. Joshua has a loyalty to Woolman."

"You're right. We'll keep it between thee and me."

Jack agreed gladly and went back to his lodgings for his working clothes.

Chapter 38
ELLEN'S PARTY

Haymaking had followed sheep shearing and at last there was leisure for ordinary folk and time for celebrations and visits.

Ellen said to her father, "Hugh is back from London and I asked Lydia to bring him in to see us, later today."

"I'll be glad to see them. Richard was coming over in any case, so we can all drink a toast together."

Richard Woolman appeared in the late afternoon. Ellen greeted him. "We are expecting company, Mr Woolman. I have asked Lydia to bring Hugh to see us."

"That's good!" Richard said. "I have hardly seen my girl since Hugh's return."

Simon was pouring some wine when they heard a knock at the door. Ellen ran to open it expecting her friends. She didn't recognize the man standing there. Her father said, "Come in lad. Are you looking for Mr Woolman?"

Richard looked up and saw it was Will Skinner.

"Yes sir, thank you, sir," Will said to Simon. He continued, "Mr Woolman, Tim thought you would be here. I'm sorry to disturb you now, but I have to ride on to Stow."

Richard drew him to one side. "What is it, Will?"

Will Skinner held out a money bag to Richard. "This is your final payment, sir. Sir Gilbert said it would be my Lord of Warwick's wish that you should be well rewarded."

"Sir Gilbert survived the battles?"

"Yes, sir."

"I am heartily glad of it. I will be sending him a gift, Will. Give him my thanks."

"I will sir, goodbye."

"God be with you, Will." He saw him to the door and they heard the horse's hooves as he set off on his journey. "Even in death, my Lord of Warwick is generous, Simon."

"Thou deserv'st thy reward, my friend."

Ellen heard a familiar voice and went to the door. Lydia and Hugh came in, full of smiles. She had not seen them together since their engagement. "Come in Lyddie. Welcome back, Hugh!"

Simon took a hand of each of them. "Welcome to you both. I have hardly had a chance to congratulate you. When will your marriage take place?"

"We go to see the Vicar on Tuesday. We hope to arrange the marriage for the middle of July," said Hugh.

Simon poured wine for them. Richard said to Simon, "I was told they couldn't wait that long but I'm glad to hear we shall have the midsummer fairs over first!"

"Mother told me she needs a month to make herself a new gown," said Hugh, "and that Lydia might find the same."

Smiling, Lydia said, "We have another ceremony to attend in the church first."

"What's that?" Ellen asked.

"Joshua and his wife have asked Hugh and me to stand godparents to their little daughter. The baptism will take place tomorrow."

"So we have even more to celebrate," Simon said.

Ellen went over to a table in the corner to pick up a plate, saying, "Lyddie, I have made a special cake for today."

"It looks very appetising!" said Lydia.

"It's very special," said Ellen. "Now that I can read,

I have been looking in the cupboard for old books and found one full of recipes from my mother's family. I have been trying out some of the ideas on Father."

"We had something very strange for dinner last Monday," said Simon. "I don't know whether the writer, the reader or the cook was to blame!" He gave Ellen an affectionate hug.

Ellen laughed and pointed out that a piece had already gone from the cake; she had eaten it to make sure it was fit for her guests. She cut several slices.

Lydia tasted the cake and pronounced it a success.

"It's all thanks to my kind teacher," Ellen said, and hugged Lydia. She handed round the cake.

Hugh went over to Richard. "Did all the pigeons arrive safely, sir?"

"Yes thank you. Your father and I were glad to have the messages. It seems you had a difficult time finding a ship."

"Yes. I hadn't expected to have to try Sandwich but in the end the fellows there were the most obliging."

"And the pigeon that went with the wool is back from Calais so we know the ship is safely in port."

Simon said, "More wine, Richard - if I may interrupt your business?"

"Yes, thank you Simon. Hugh was asking after my pigeons. They're glad to be back on wool business instead of reporting army manoeuvres!"

"I've been telling Hugh about our young birds," said Lydia. "The chicks hatched in the spring have been making successful training flights. Joshua certainly has a way with them."

They heard another knock on the door. Simon opened it to find John Plentey standing there, Mrs Plentey just behind him. She hung back shyly. She usually left visits of this kind to her husband and was surprised to see Hugh there.

"Come in, John," said Simon. "And Mrs Plentey

too. Come in, my dear." Ellen came over to welcome them.

"We were just taking a little walk, Simon," said John. "I thought to combine business with pleasure. Such a beautiful evening."

"We mustn't interrupt your party," said Mrs Plentey.

Simon insisted their walk could wait. "Come and join our celebration. Can your business wait too, John?"

But John Plentey needed to carry out his errand. He took Simon to one side while Ellen plied Mrs Plentey with wine and cake. Lydia and Hugh joined them and she was soon chattering happily, her shyness forgotten.

"Simon, I have a little gift for the church. My wife and I would like you as churchwarden to accept this purse in thankfulness for the peace of England and in memory of our son, Robert."

Simon was touched and took the little purse. "I'm grateful, John. I can say that on behalf of all the churchwardens. Tom showed me a sheaf of unpaid bills this morning."

Richard couldn't help overhearing. "Simon, if John can give more money to the church then so can I!" With a wry smile, he handed over the larger purse that Will Skinner had brought him.

1484

Epilogue

Anne Neville is Queen of England. She was married to Richard, Duke of Gloucester the year after the Battle of Tewkesbury. He was crowned King Richard III last year. Anne is back at her beloved Middleham Castle. She is not often well enough to travel with the king. Her mother, the Countess of Warwick, has recently come to be with her. Anne's only child, another Prince Edward, died a few months ago at the age of eleven. King Richard has no heir.

Isabel Neville died seven years ago. She left two children. Her husband, George Duke of Clarence, was charged with treason soon after Isabel's death and was executed in the Tower of London. He had defied his brother King Edward IV again and again. Lydia did see Isabel once more, a few months before her death. She was not very well but was struggling on bravely.

Lydia has not seen Anne again, not since the day she left Middleham. Anne writes every year on Barnet's anniversary. Always she speaks of meeting again when one day the king needs to ride from Oxford to Gloucester.

Tom, the Foreman, died last year. He retired when the north aisle of the church was finished. He lived to see the rest of the building work completed. Lydia and Hugh are raising a large family of children. Ellen too is married with children. Their parents are ageing but still in good health. Mrs Plentey, Lydia's mother-in-law, asks her every week if she has heard from the queen.

List of Characters

Isabel Neville

Anne Neville

The Countess of Warwick, their mother

Lydia Woolman,	Companion to Isabel
Richard Woolman,	Lydia's father, Wool Merchant in Northleach
Simon Trencher,	Baker and Churchwarden
Ellen Trencher,	his daughter
John Plentey,	Wool Merchant
Mrs Plentey,	his wife
Robert, Hugh, }	their sons
Geoffrey Langbroke,	the Vicar of Northleach
Adam Fry,	London Wool Merchant and cousin to Woolman
Tom,	Building Foreman at the church
Joshua,	Mason and part-time Servant to Woolman
Margery,	Housekeeper to Woolman
Tim,	Servant to Woolman
Cuthbert, Jack, }	Labourers
Rupert,	Master Mason from Windsor

Sir Gilbert de Villepion,	Agent of the Earl of Warwick
William Skinner	his Deputy

THE ROYAL FAMILY up to March 1471

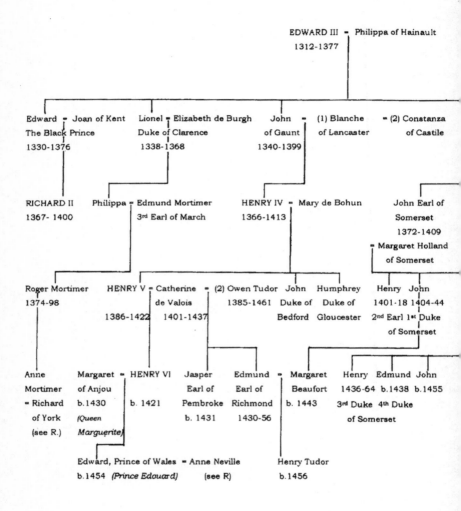

King Edward III had 5 sons;
none became King

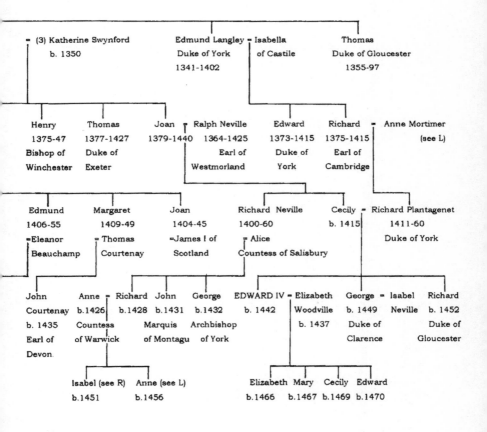

Acknowledgements

My thanks go to the following:

My sister, Susanna Scrivener, for her encouragement, and help with grammar and punctuation.

The Staff of the Mobile Library based at Moreton-in-Marsh, Glos., who brought me books for over thirty years.

Derek Stevens, author, John Nash, director, Robin Greenwood, producer, and all those who helped to stage *Shirt of Fire* in Gloucester Cathedral in 1989, for inspiration.

Phil Skipper, for transferring the text from an old word-processor to a new laptop.

The Staff of:
  The Gloucestershire Record Office
  Coventry Visitor Centre
  Warwick Castle
  Burford Museum
The late Ralph H. C. Davis, Universities of Oxford and Birmingham
Alan Bartlett, University of Durham
The late Anthony Hodge
Tim Porter
Sue Colverd
Jean Plant
John Dixon and Steve Goodchild of Tewkesbury Historical Society
Peter Bryant and Mark Edwards of the Royal Pigeon Racing Association, Cheltenham
My family for support, suggestions and help with the computer

In and around Northleach:
  Enid Sly and Joan Smith of Northleach Historical
      Society
  The late Llewellyn Sly
  The late William Fallows
  Philip Brown
  John Pegrum
  The late Selina Ballance
  The late John Fothergill
  Jacquie Crago
  Dick Woodger
  Patsi Rainey

Bibliography

The Cely Letters 1472-1488, Alison Hanham, Early English Text Society

The Wool Trade in English Medieval History, Eileen Power, OUP

The Wool-Pack, Cynthia Harnett, Puffin

The Merchant of Prato, Iris Origo, London, Folio Society

Cotswold Churches, David Verey, Batsford

A Catalogue of Masons' Marks as an Aid to Architectural History, R. H. C. Davis,

Journal of the British Archaeological Association

The Will of John Fortey, 1458

The Master Builders, John Harvey, Thames & Hudson

Building in England down to 1540, L. F. Salzman, Clarendon Press

Engineering in the Ancient World, J. G. Landels, Constable

The Voices of Morebath: Reformation and Rebellion in an English Village, Eamon Duffy, Yale University Press

The Bible, in particular *The Gospel of St John* & *The Acts of the Apostles*

Steps in a Large Room: A Quaker explores the Monastic Tradition, Christopher Holdsworth, Quaker Home Service

Lancaster and York: The Wars of the Roses, Alison Weir, Jonathan Cape

The Red Rose and the White: The Wars of the Roses 1453-1487, John Sadler, Longman

The Military Campaigns of the Wars of the Roses, Philip A. Haigh, Sutton Publishing

The Wars of the Roses, Charles Ross, Thames & Hudson

Conflict and Stability in Fifteenth Century England, J. R. Lander, Ontario

Bosworth Field, A. L. Rouse, Macmillan

The Plantagenets, John Harvey, Batsford

This Sun of York: A Biography of Edward IV, Mary Clive, Macmillan

Edward IV, Charles Ross, Eyre Methuen

Warwick the Kingmaker, Paul Kendall, Allen & Unwin

The Last of the Barons, Brenda Clarke, Severn House

Margaret of Anjou, Philippe Erlanger, Orion

The Spider King, a biographical novel of Louis XI of France, Lawrence Schoonover, Collins

An Unknown Welshman, Jean Stubbs, Macmillan

Middleham Castle, English Heritage Visitor Guide

The Battle of Tewkesbury May 4th 1471, B. Linnell, Treoc Press

The Cotswold Sheep, Edited by L. V. Gibbings, Geerings of Ashford Ltd.

Tackle Pigeon Racing This Way, Harold Blunt, Stanley Paul, London

Racing Pigeons, Colin Osman, Faber